New Chronicles of Rebecca

Kate Douglas Wiggin

New Chronicles of Rebecca

ISBN: 979-8-88830-649-9

CONTENTS

FIRST CHRONICLE

JACK O'LANTERN

I

Miss Miranda Sawyer's old-fashioned garden was the pleasantest spot in Riverboro on a sunny July morning. The rich color of the brick house gleamed and glowed through the shade of the elms and maples. Luxuriant hop-vines clambered up the lightning rods and water spouts, hanging their delicate clusters here and there in graceful profusion. Woodbine transformed the old shed and tool house to things of beauty, and the flower beds themselves were the prettiest and most fragrant in all the countryside. A row of dahlias ran directly around the garden spot,—dahlias scarlet, gold, and variegated. In the very centre was a round plot where the upturned faces of a thousand pansies smiled amid their leaves, and in the four corners were triangular blocks of sweet phlox over which the butterflies fluttered unceasingly. In the spaces between ran a riot of portulaca and nasturtiums, while in the more regular, shell-bordered beds grew spirea and gillyflowers, mignonette, marigolds, and clove pinks.

Back of the barn and encroaching on the edge of the hay field was a grove of sweet clover whose white feathery tips fairly bent under the assaults of the bees, while banks of aromatic mint and thyme drank in the sunshine and sent it out again into the summer air, warm, and deliciously odorous.

The hollyhocks were Miss Sawyer's pride, and they grew in a stately line beneath the four kitchen windows, their tapering tips set thickly with gay satin circlets of pink or lavender or crimson.

"They grow something like steeples," thought little Rebecca Randall, who was weeding the bed, "and the flat, round flowers are like rosettes; but steeples wouldn't be studded with rosettes, so if you were writing about them in a composition you'd have to give up one or the other, and I think I'll give up the steeples:—

Gay little hollyhock
Lifting your head,
Sweetly rosetted
Out from your bed.

It's a pity the hollyhock isn't really little, instead of steepling up to the window top, but I can't say, 'Gay TALL hollyhock.'... I might have it 'Lines to a Hollyhock in May,' for then it would be small; but oh, no! I forgot; in May it wouldn't be blooming, and it's so pretty to say that its head is 'sweetly rosetted'... I wish the teacher wasn't away; she would like 'sweetly rosetted,' and she would like to hear me recite 'Roll on, thou deep and dark blue ocean, roll!' that I learned out of Aunt Jane's Byron; the rolls come booming out of it just like the waves at the beach.... I could make nice compositions now, everything is blooming so, and it's so warm and sunny and happy outdoors. Miss Dearborn told me to write something in my thought book every single day, and I'll begin this very night when I go to bed."

Rebecca Rowena Randall, the little niece of the brick-house ladies, and at present sojourning there for purposes of board, lodging, education, and incidentally such discipline and chastening as might ultimately produce moral excellence,—Rebecca Randall had a passion for the rhyme and rhythm of poetry. From her earliest childhood words had always been to her what dolls and toys are to other children, and now at twelve she amused herself with phrases and sentences and images as her schoolmates played with the pieces of their dissected puzzles. If the heroine of a story took a "cursory glance" about her "apartment," Rebecca would shortly ask her Aunt Jane to take a "cursory glance" at her oversewing or hemming; if the villain "aided and abetted" someone in committing a crime, she would before long request the pleasure of "aiding and abetting" in dishwashing or bedmaking. Sometimes she used the borrowed phrases unconsciously; sometimes she brought them into the conversation with an intense sense of

2

pleasure in their harmony or appropriateness; for a beautiful word or sentence had the same effect upon her imagination as a fragrant nosegay, a strain of music, or a brilliant sunset.

"How are you gettin' on, Rebecca Rowena?" called a peremptory voice from within.

"Pretty good, Aunt Miranda; only I wish flowers would ever come up as thick as this pigweed and plantain and sorrel. What MAKES weeds be thick and flowers be thin?—I just happened to be stopping to think a minute when you looked out."

"You think considerable more than you weed, I guess, by appearances. How many times have you peeked into that humming bird's nest? Why don't you work all to once and play all to once, like other folks?"

"I don't know," the child answered, confounded by the question, and still more by the apparent logic back of it. "I don't know, Aunt Miranda, but when I'm working outdoors such a Saturday morning as this, the whole creation just screams to me to stop it and come and play."

"Well, you needn't go if it does!" responded her aunt sharply. "It don't scream to me when I'm rollin' out these doughnuts, and it wouldn't to you if your mind was on your duty."

Rebecca's little brown hands flew in and out among the weeds as she thought rebelliously: "Creation *wouldn't* scream to Aunt Miranda; it would know she wouldn't come."

> Scream on, thou bright and gay creation, scream!
> 'Tis not Miranda that will hear thy cry!

Oh, such funny, nice things come into my head out here by myself, I do wish I could run up and put them down in my thought book before I forget them, but Aunt Miranda wouldn't like me to leave off weeding:—

> Rebecca was weeding the hollyhock bed
> When wonderful thoughts came into her head.
> Her aunt was occupied with the rolling pin
> And the thoughts of her mind were common and thin.

3

That wouldn't do because it's mean to Aunt Miranda, and anyway it isn't good. I MUST crawl under the syringa shade a minute, it's so hot, and anybody has to stop working once in a while, just to get their breath, even if they weren't making poetry.

Rebecca was weeding the hollyhock bed When marvelous thoughts came into her head. Miranda was wielding the rolling pin And thoughts at such times seemed to her as a sin.

How pretty the hollyhock rosettes look from down here on the sweet, smelly ground!

"Let me see what would go with rosetting. *Aiding and abetting, petting, hen-setting, fretting,*—there's nothing very nice, but I can make fretting' do.

> *Cheered by Rowena's petting,*
> *The flowers are rosetting,*
> *But Aunt Miranda's fretting*
> *Doth somewhat cloud the day."*

Suddenly the sound of wagon wheels broke the silence and then a voice called out—a voice that could not wait until the feet that belonged to it reached the spot: "Miss Saw-YER! Father's got to drive over to North Riverboro on an errand, and please can Rebecca go, too, as it's Saturday morning and vacation besides?"

Rebecca sprang out from under the syringa bush, eyes flashing with delight as only Rebecca's eyes *could* flash, her face one luminous circle of joyous anticipation. She clapped her grubby hands, and dancing up and down, cried: "May I, Aunt Miranda—can I, Aunt Jane—can I, Aunt Miranda-Jane? I'm more than half through the bed."

"If you finish your weeding tonight before sundown I s'pose you can go, so long as Mr. Perkins has been good enough to ask you," responded Miss Sawyer reluctantly. "Take off that gingham apron and wash your hands clean at the pump. You ain't be'n out o' bed but two hours an' your head looks as rough as if you'd slep' in it. That comes from layin' on the ground same as a caterpillar.

4

Smooth your hair down with your hands an' p'r'aps Emma Jane can braid it as you go along the road. Run up and get your second-best hair ribbon out o' your upper drawer and put on your shade hat. No, you can't wear your coral chain—jewelry ain't appropriate in the morning. How long do you cal'late to be gone, Emma Jane?"

"I don't know. Father's just been sent for to see about a sick woman over to North Riverboro. She's got to go to the poor farm."

This fragment of news speedily brought Miss Sawyer, and her sister Jane as well, to the door, which commanded a view of Mr. Perkins and his wagon. Mr. Perkins, the father of Rebecca's bosom friend, was primarily a blacksmith, and secondarily a selectman and an overseer of the poor, a man therefore possessed of wide and varied information.

"Who is it that's sick?" inquired Miranda.

"A woman over to North Riverboro."

"What's the trouble?"

"Can't say."

"Stranger?'

"Yes, and no; she's that wild daughter of old Nate Perry that used to live up towards Moderation. You remember she ran away to work in the factory at Milltown and married a do—nothin' fellow by the name o' John Winslow?"

"Yes; well, where is he? Why don't he take care of her?"

"They ain't worked well in double harness. They've been rovin' round the country, livin' a month here and a month there wherever they could get work and house-room. They quarreled a couple o' weeks ago and he left her. She and the little boy kind o' camped out in an old loggin' cabin back in the woods and she took in washin' for a spell; then she got terrible sick and ain't expected to live."

"Who's been nursing her?" inquired Miss Jane.

"Lizy Ann Dennett, that lives nearest neighbor to the cabin; but I guess she's tired out bein' good Samaritan. Anyways, she sent word this mornin' that nobody can't seem to find John Winslow; that there ain't no relations, and the town's got to be responsible, so I'm goin' over to see how the land lays. Climb in, Rebecca. You an' Emmy Jane crowd back on the cushion an' I'll set forrard. That's the trick! Now we're off!"

5

"Dear, dear!" sighed Jane Sawyer as the sisters walked back into the brick house. "I remember once seeing Sally Perry at meeting. She was a handsome girl, and I'm sorry she's come to grief."

"If she'd kep' on goin' to meetin' an' hadn't looked at the men folks she might a' be'n earnin' an honest livin' this minute," said Miranda. "Men folks are at the bottom of everything wrong in this world," she continued, unconsciously reversing the verdict of history.

"Then we ought to be a happy and contented community here in Riverboro," replied Jane, "as there's six women to one man."

"If 't was sixteen to one we'd be all the safer," responded Miranda grimly, putting the doughnuts in a brown crock in the cellar-way and slamming the door.

II

The Perkins horse and wagon rumbled along over the dusty country road, and after a discreet silence, maintained as long as human flesh could endure, Rebecca remarked sedately:

"It's a sad errand for such a shiny morning, isn't it, Mr. Perkins?"

"Plenty o' trouble in the world, Rebecky, shiny mornin's an' all," that good man replied. "If you want a bed to lay on, a roof over your head, an' food to eat, you've got to work for em. If I hadn't a' labored early an' late, learned my trade, an' denied myself when I was young, I might a' be'n a pauper layin' sick in a loggin' cabin, stead o' bein' an overseer o' the poor an' selectman drivin' along to take the pauper to the poor farm."

"People that are mortgaged don't have to go to the poor farm, do they, Mr. Perkins?" asked Rebecca, with a shiver of fear as she remembered her home farm at Sunnybrook and the debt upon it; a debt which had lain like a shadow over her childhood.

"Bless your soul, no; not unless they fail to pay up; but Sal Perry an' her husband hadn't got fur enough along in life to *be* mortgaged. You have to own something before you can mortgage it."

Rebecca's heart bounded as she learned that a mortgage represented a certain stage in worldly prosperity.

"Well," she said, sniffing in the fragrance of the new-mown hay and growing hopeful as she did so; "maybe the sick woman will be better such a beautiful day, and maybe the husband will come back to make it up and say he's sorry, and sweet content will reign in the humble habitation that was once the scene of poverty, grief, and despair. That's how it came out in a story I'm reading."

"I hain't noticed that life comes out like stories very much," responded the pessimistic blacksmith, who, as Rebecca privately thought, had read less than half a dozen books in his long and prosperous career.

A drive of three or four miles brought the party to a patch of woodland where many of the tall pines had been hewn the previous winter. The roof of a ramshackle hut was outlined against a background of young birches, and a rough path made in hauling the logs to the main road led directly to its door.

As they drew near the figure of a woman approached—Mrs. Lizy Ann Dennett, in a gingham dress, with a calico apron over her head.

"Good morning, Mr. Perkins," said the woman, who looked tired and irritable. "I'm real glad you come right over, for she took worse after I sent you word, and she's dead."

Dead! The word struck heavily and mysteriously on the children's ears. Dead! And their young lives, just begun, stretched on and on, all decked, like hope, in living green. Dead! And all the rest of the world reveling in strength. Dead! With all the daisies and buttercups waving in the fields and the men heaping the mown grass into fragrant cocks or tossing it into heavily laden carts. Dead! With the brooks tinkling after the summer showers, with the potatoes and corn blossoming, the birds singing for joy, and every little insect humming and chirping, adding its note to the blithe chorus of warm, throbbing life.

"I was all alone with her. She passed away suddenly jest about break o' day," said Lizy Ann Dennett.

7

*"Her soul passed upward to its God
Just at the break of day."*

These words came suddenly into Rebecca's mind from a tiny chamber where such things were wont to lie quietly until something brought them to the surface. She could not remember whether she had heard them at a funeral or read them in the hymn book or made them up "out of her own head," but she was so thrilled with the idea of dying just as the dawn was breaking that she scarcely heard Mrs. Dennett's conversation.

"I sent for Aunt Beulah Day, an' she's be'n here an' laid her out," continued the long suffering Lizy Ann. "She ain't got any folks, an' John Winslow ain't never had any as far back as I can remember. She belongs to your town and you'll have to bury her and take care of Jacky—that's the boy. He's seventeen months old, a bright little feller, the image o' John, but I can't keep him another day. I'm all wore out; my own baby's sick, mother's rheumatiz is extry bad, and my husband's comin' home tonight from his week's work. If he finds a child o' John Winslow's under his roof I can't say what would happen; you'll have to take him back with you to the poor farm."

"I can't take him up there this afternoon," objected Mr. Perkins.

"Well, then, keep him over Sunday yourself; he's good as a kitten. John Winslow'll hear o' Sal's death sooner or later, unless he's gone out of the state altogether, an' when he knows the boy's at the poor farm, I kind o' think he'll come and claim him. Could you drive me over to the village to see about the coffin, and would you children be afraid to stay here alone for a spell?" she asked, turning to the girls.

"Afraid?" they both echoed uncomprehendingly.

Lizy Ann and Mr. Perkins, perceiving that the fear of a dead presence had not entered the minds of Rebecca or Emma Jane, said nothing, but drove off together, counseling them not to stray far away from the cabin and promising to be back in an hour.

There was not a house within sight, either looking up or down the shady road, and the two girls stood hand in hand, watching the wagon out of sight; then they sat down quietly under a tree, feeling

8

all at once a nameless depression hanging over their gay summer-morning spirits.

It was very still in the woods; just the chirp of a grasshopper now and then, or the note of a bird, or the click of a far-distant mowing machine.

"We're *watching*!" whispered Emma Jane. "They watched with Gran'pa Perkins, and there was a great funeral and two ministers. He left two thousand dollars in the bank and a store full of goods, and a paper thing you could cut tickets off of twice a year, and they were just like money."

"They watched with my little sister Mira, too," said Rebecca. "You remember when she died, and I went home to Sunnybrook Farm? It was winter time, but she was covered with evergreen and white pinks, and there was singing."

"There won't be any funeral or ministers or singing here, will there? Isn't that awful?"

"I s'pose not; and oh, Emma Jane, no flowers either. We might get those for her if there's nobody else to do it."

"Would you dare put them on to her?" asked Emma Jane, in a hushed voice.

"I don't know; I can't tell; it makes me shiver, but, of course, we *could* do it if we were the only friends she had. Let's look into the cabin first and be perfectly sure that there aren't any. Are you afraid?"

"N-no; I guess not. I looked at Gran'pa Perkins, and he was just the same as ever."

At the door of the hut Emma Jane's courage suddenly departed. She held back shuddering and refused either to enter or look in. Rebecca shuddered too, but kept on, drawn by an insatiable curiosity about life and death, an overmastering desire to know and feel and understand the mysteries of existence, a hunger for knowledge and experience at all hazards and at any cost.

Emma Jane hurried softly away from the felt terrors of the cabin, and after two or three minutes of utter silence Rebecca issued from the open door, her sensitive face pale and woe-begone, the ever-ready tears raining down her cheeks. She ran toward the edge

9

of the wood, sinking down by Emma Jane's side, and covering her eyes, sobbed with excitement:

"Oh, Emma Jane, she hasn't got a flower, and she's so tired and sad-looking, as if she'd been hurt and hurt and never had any good times, and there's a weeny, weeny baby side of her. Oh, I wish I hadn't gone in!"

Emma Jane blenched for an instant. "Mrs. Dennett never said *there was two dead ones! Isn't that dreadful*? But," she continued, her practical common sense coming to the rescue, "you've been in once and it's all over; it won't be so bad when you take in the flowers because you'll be used to it. The goldenrod hasn't begun to bud, so there's nothing to pick but daisies. Shall I make a long rope of them, as I did for the schoolroom?"

"Yes," said Rebecca, wiping her eyes and still sobbing. "Yes, that's the prettiest, and if we put it all round her like a frame, the undertaker couldn't be so cruel as to throw it away, even if she is a pauper, because it will look so beautiful. From what the Sunday school lessons say, she's only asleep now, and when she wakes up she'll be in heaven."

"*There's another place*," said Emma Jane, in an orthodox and sepulchral whisper, as she took her ever-present ball of crochet cotton from her pocket and began to twine the whiteweed blossoms into a rope.

"Oh, well!" Rebecca replied with the easy theology that belonged to her temperament. "They simply couldn't send her *down there* with that little weeny baby. Who'd take care of it? You know page six of the catechism says the only companions of the wicked after death are their father the devil and all the other evil angels; it wouldn't be any place to bring up a baby."

"Whenever and wherever she wakes up, I hope she won't know that the big baby is going to the poor farm. I wonder where he is?"

"Perhaps over to Mrs. Dennett's house. She didn't seem sorry a bit, did she?"

"No, but I suppose she's tired sitting up and nursing a stranger. Mother wasn't sorry when Gran'pa Perkins died; she couldn't be,

10

for he was cross all the time and had to be fed like a child. Why *are* you crying again, Rebecca?"

"Oh, I don't know, I can't tell, Emma Jane! Only I don't want to die and have no funeral or singing and nobody sorry for me! I just couldn't bear it!"

"Neither could I," Emma Jane responded sympathetically; "but p'r'aps if we're real good and die young before we have to be fed, they will be sorry. I do wish you could write some poetry for her as you did for Alice Robinson's canary bird, only still better, of course, like that you read me out of your thought book."

"I could, easy enough," exclaimed Rebecca, somewhat consoled by the idea that her rhyming faculty could be of any use in such an emergency. "Though I don't know but it would be kind of bold to do it. I'm all puzzled about how people get to heaven after they're buried. I can't understand it a bit; but if the poetry is on her, what if that should go, too? And how could I write anything good enough to be read out loud in heaven?"

"A little piece of paper couldn't get to heaven; it just couldn't," asserted Emma Jane decisively. "It would be all blown to pieces and dried up. And nobody knows that the angels can read writing, anyway."

"They must be as educated as we are, and more so, too," agreed Rebecca. "They must be more than just dead people, or else why should they have wings? But I'll go off and write something while you finish the rope; it's lucky you brought your crochet cotton and I my lead pencil."

In fifteen or twenty minutes she returned with some lines written on a scrap of brown wrapping paper. Standing soberly by Emma Jane, she said, preparing to read them aloud: "They're not good; I was afraid your father'd come back before I finished, and the first verse sounds exactly like the funeral hymns in the church book. I couldn't call her Sally Winslow; it didn't seem nice when I didn't know her and she is dead, so I thought if I said friend' it would show she had somebody to be sorry.

"This friend of ours has died and gone
From us to heaven to live.

11

If she has sinned against Thee, Lord,
We pray Thee, Lord, forgive.

"Her husband runneth far away
And knoweth not she's dead.
Oh, bring him back—ere tis too late—
To mourn beside her bed.

"And if perchance it can't be so,
Be to the children kind;
The weeny one that goes with her,
The other left behind."

"I think that's perfectly elegant!" exclaimed Emma Jane, kissing Rebecca fervently. "You are the smartest girl in the whole State of Maine, and it sounds like a minister's prayer. I wish we could save up and buy a printing machine. Then I could learn to print what you write and we'd be partners like father and Bill Moses. Shall you sign it with your name like we do our school compositions?"

"No," said Rebecca soberly. "I certainly shan't sign it, not knowing where it's going or who'll read it. I shall just hide it in the flowers, and whoever finds it will guess that there wasn't any minister or singing, or gravestone, or anything, so somebody just did the best they could."

III

The tired mother with the "weeny baby" on her arm lay on a long carpenter's bench, her earthly journey over, and when Rebecca stole in and placed the flowery garland all along the edge of the rude bier, death suddenly took on a more gracious and benign aspect. It was only a child's sympathy and intuition that softened the rigors of the sad moment, but poor, wild Sal Winslow, in her frame of daisies, looked as if she were missed a little by an unfriendly world; while the weeny baby, whose heart had fallen asleep almost as soon as it had learned to beat, the weeny baby, with Emma Jane's nosegay of buttercups in its tiny wrinkled hand, smiled as if it might have been loved and longed for and mourned.

"We've done all we can now without a minister," whispered Rebecca. "We could sing, God is ever good' out of the Sunday school song book, but I'm afraid somebody would hear us and think we were gay and happy. What's that?"

A strange sound broke the stillness; a gurgle, a yawn, a merry little call. The two girls ran in the direction from which it came, and there, on an old coat, in a clump of goldenrod bushes, lay a child just waking from a refreshing nap.

"It's the other baby that Lizy Ann Dennett told about!" cried Emma Jane.

"Isn't he beautiful!" exclaimed Rebecca. "Come straight to me!" and she stretched out her arms.

The child struggled to its feet, and tottered, wavering, toward the warm welcome of the voice and eyes. Rebecca was all mother, and her maternal instincts had been well developed in the large family in which she was next to the eldest. She had always confessed that there were perhaps a trifle too many babies at Sunnybrook Farm, but, nevertheless, had she ever heard it, she would have stood loyally by the Japanese proverb: "Whether brought forth upon the mountain or in the field, it matters nothing; more than a treasure of one thousand ryo a baby precious is."

"You darling thing!" she crooned, as she caught and lifted the child. "You look just like a Jack-o'-lantern."

The boy was clad in a yellow cotton dress, very full and stiff. His hair was of such a bright gold, and so sleek and shiny, that he looked like a fair, smooth little pumpkin. He had wide blue eyes full of laughter, a neat little vertical nose, a neat little horizontal mouth with his few neat little teeth showing very plainly, and on the whole Rebecca's figure of speech was not so wide of the mark.

"Oh, Emma Jane! Isn't he too lovely to go to the poor farm? If only we were married we could keep him and say nothing and nobody would know the difference! Now that the Simpsons have gone away there isn't a single baby in Riverboro, and only one in

13

Edgewood. It's a perfect shame, but I can't do anything; you remember Aunt Miranda wouldn't let me have the Simpson baby when I wanted to borrow her just for one rainy Sunday."

"My mother won't keep him, so it's no use to ask her; she says most every day she's glad we're grown up, and she thanks the Lord there wasn't but two of us."

"And Mrs. Peter Meserve is too nervous," Rebecca went on, taking the village houses in turn; "and Mrs. Robinson is too neat."

"People don't seem to like any but their own babies," observed Emma Jane.

"Well, I can't understand it," Rebecca answered. "A baby's a baby, I should think, whose ever it is! Miss Dearborn is coming back Monday; I wonder if she'd like it? She has nothing to do out of school, and we could borrow it all the time!"

"I don't think it would seem very genteel for a young lady like Miss Dearborn, who 'boards round,' to take a baby from place to place," objected Emma Jane.

"Perhaps not," agreed Rebecca despondently, "but I think if we haven't got any—any—*private* babies in Riverboro we ought to have one for the town, and all have a share in it. We've got a town hall and a town lamp post and a town watering trough. Things are so uneven! One house like mine at Sunnybrook, brimful of children, and the very next one empty! The only way to fix them right would be to let all the babies that ever are belong to all the grown-up people that ever are,—just divide them up, you know, if they'd go round. Oh, I have a thought! Don't you believe Aunt Sarah Cobb would keep him? She carries flowers to the graveyard every little while, and once she took me with her. There's a marble cross, and it says: *sacred to the memory of Sarah Ellen, beloved child of Sarah and Jeremiah Cobb, aged 17 months.* Why, that's another reason; Mrs. Dennett says this one is seventeen months. There's five of us left at the farm without me, but if we were only nearer to Riverboro, how quick mother would let in one more!"

"We might see what father thinks, and that would settle it," said Emma Jane. "Father doesn't think very sudden, but he thinks awful strong. If we don't bother him, and find a place ourselves for

14

the baby, perhaps he'll be willing. He's coming now; I hear the wheels."

Lizy Ann Dennett volunteered to stay and perform the last rites with the undertaker, and Jack-o'-lantern, with his slender wardrobe tied in a bandanna handkerchief, was lifted into the wagon by the reluctant Mr. Perkins, and jubilantly held by Rebecca in her lap. Mr. Perkins drove off as speedily as possible, being heartily sick of the whole affair, and thinking wisely that the little girls had already seen and heard more than enough of the seamy side of life that morning.

Discussion concerning Jack-o'-lantern's future was prudently deferred for a quarter of an hour, and then Mr. Perkins was mercilessly pelted with arguments against the choice of the poor farm as a place of residence for a baby.

"His father is sure to come back some time, Mr. Perkins," urged Rebecca. "He couldn't leave this beautiful thing forever; and if Emma Jane and I can persuade Mrs. Cobb to keep him a little while, would you care?"

No; on reflection Mr. Perkins did not care. He merely wanted a quiet life and enough time left over from the public service to attend to his blacksmith's shop; so instead of going home over the same road by which they came he crossed the bridge into Edgewood and dropped the children at the long lane which led to the Cobb house.

Mrs. Cobb, "Aunt Sarah" to the whole village, sat by the window looking for Uncle Jerry, who would soon be seen driving the noon stage to the post office over the hill. She always had an eye out for Rebecca, too, for ever since the child had been a passenger on Mr. Cobb's stagecoach, making the eventful trip from her home farm to the brick house in Riverboro in his company, she had been a constant visitor and the joy of the quiet household. Emma Jane, too, was a well-known figure in the lane, but the strange baby was in the nature of a surprise—a surprise somewhat modified by the fact that Rebecca was a dramatic personage and more liable to appear in conjunction with curious outriders, comrades, and retainers than the ordinary Riverboro child. She had run away from the too stern discipline of the brick house on one occasion, and had been

15

persuaded to return by Uncle Jerry. She had escorted a wandering organ grinder to their door and begged a lodging for him on a rainy night; so on the whole there was nothing amazing about the coming procession.

The little party toiled up to the hospitable door, and Mrs. Cobb came out to meet them.

Rebecca was spokesman. Emma Jane's talent did not lie in eloquent speech, but it would have been a valiant and a fluent child indeed who could have usurped Rebecca's privileges and tendencies in this direction, language being her native element, and words of assorted sizes springing spontaneously to her lips.

"Aunt Sarah, dear," she said, plumping Jack-o'-lantern down on the grass as she pulled his dress over his feet and smoothed his hair becomingly, "will you please not say a word till I get through—as it's very important you should know everything before you answer yes or no? This is a baby named Jacky Winslow, and I think he looks like a Jack-o'-lantern. His mother has just died over to North Riverboro, all alone, excepting for Mrs. Lizy Ann Dennett, and there was another little weeny baby that died with her, and Emma Jane and I put flowers around them and did the best we could. The father—that's John Winslow—quarreled with the mother—that was Sal Perry on the Moderation Road—and ran away and left her. So he doesn't know his wife and the weeny baby are dead. And the town has got to bury them because they can't find the father right off quick, and Jacky has got to go to the poor farm this afternoon. And it seems an awful shame to take him up to that lonesome place with those old people that can't amuse him, and if Emma Jane and Alice Robinson and I take most all the care of him we thought perhaps you and Uncle Jerry would keep him just for a little while. You've got a cow and a turn-up bedstead, you know," she hurried on insinuatingly, "and there's hardly any pleasure as cheap as more babies where there's ever been any before, for baby carriages and trundle beds and cradles don't wear out, and there's always clothes left over from the old baby to begin the new one on. Of course, we can collect enough things to start Jacky, so he won't be much trouble or expense; and anyway, he's past the most troublesome age and you won't have to be up nights

16

with him, and he isn't afraid of anybody or anything, as you can see by his just sitting there laughing and sucking his thumb, though he doesn't know what's going to become of him. And he's just seventeen months old like dear little Sarah Ellen in the graveyard, and we thought we ought to give you the refusal of him before he goes to the poor farm, and what do you think about it? Because it's near my dinner time and Aunt Miranda will keep me in the whole afternoon if I'm late, and I've got to finish weeding the hollyhock bed before sundown."

IV

Mrs. Cobb had enjoyed a considerable period of reflection during this monologue, and Jacky had not used the time unwisely, offering several unconscious arguments and suggestions to the matter under discussion; lurching over on the greensward and righting himself with a chuckle, kicking his bare feet about in delight at the sunshine and groping for his toes with arms too short to reach them, the movement involving an entire upsetting of equilibrium followed by more chuckles.

Coming down the last of the stone steps, Sarah Ellen's mother regarded the baby with interest and sympathy.

"Poor little mite!" she said; "that doesn't know what he's lost and what's going to happen to him. Seems to me we might keep him a spell till we're sure his father's deserted him for good. Want to come to Aunt Sarah, baby?"

Jack-o'-lantern turned from Rebecca and Emma Jane and regarded the kind face gravely; then he held out both his hands and Mrs. Cobb, stooping, gathered him like a harvest. Being lifted into her arms, he at once tore her spectacles from her nose and laughed aloud. Taking them from him gently, she put them on again, and set him in the cushioned rocking chair under the lilac bushes beside the steps. Then she took one of his soft hands in hers and patted it, and fluttered her fingers like birds before his eyes, and snapped

17

them like castanets, remembering all the arts she had lavished upon "Sarah Ellen, aged seventeen months," years and years ago.

Motherless baby and babyless mother,
Bring them together to love one another.

Rebecca knew nothing of this couplet, but she saw clearly enough that her case was won.

"The boy must be hungry; when was he fed last?" asked Mrs. Cobb. "Just stay a second longer while I get him some morning's milk; then you run home to your dinners and I'll speak to Mr. Cobb this afternoon. Of course, we can keep the baby for a week or two till we see what happens. Land! He ain't goin' to be any more trouble than a wax doll! I guess he ain't been used to much attention, and that kind's always the easiest to take care of."

At six o'clock that evening Rebecca and Emma Jane flew up the hill and down the lane again, waving their hands to the dear old couple who were waiting for them in the usual place, the back piazza where they had sat so many summers in a blessed companionship never marred by an unloving word.

"Where's Jacky?" called Rebecca breathlessly, her voice always outrunning her feet.

"Go up to my chamber, both of you, if you want to see," smiled Mrs. Cobb, "only don't wake him up."

The girls went softly up the stairs into Aunt Sarah's room. There, in the turn-up bedstead that had been so long empty, slept Jack-o'-lantern, in blissful unconsciousness of the doom he had so lately escaped. His nightgown and pillow case were clean and fragrant with lavender, but they were both as yellow as saffron, for they had belonged to Sarah Ellen.

"I wish his mother could see him!" whispered Emma Jane.

"You can't tell; it's all puzzly about heaven, and perhaps she does," said Rebecca, as they turned reluctantly from the fascinating scene and stole down to the piazza.

It was a beautiful and a happy summer that year, and every day it was filled with blissful plays and still more blissful duties. On the Monday after Jack-o'-lantern's arrival in Edgewood Rebecca founded the Riverboro Aunts Association. The Aunts were Rebecca, Emma Jane, Alice Robinson, and Minnie Smellie, and each of the first three promised to labor for and amuse the visiting baby for two days a week, Minnie Smellie, who lived at some distance from the Cobbs, making herself responsible for Saturday afternoons.

Minnie Smellie was not a general favorite among the Riverboro girls, and it was only in an unprecedented burst of magnanimity that they admitted her into the rites of fellowship, Rebecca hugging herself secretly at the thought, that as Minnie gave only the leisure time of one day a week, she could not be called a "full" Aunt. There had been long and bitter feuds between the two children during Rebecca's first summer in Riverboro, but since Mrs. Smellie had told her daughter that one more quarrel would invite a punishment so terrible that it could only be hinted at vaguely, and Miss Miranda Sawyer had remarked that any niece of hers who couldn't get along peaceable with the neighbors had better go back to the seclusion of a farm where there weren't any, hostilities had been veiled, and a suave and diplomatic relationship had replaced the former one, which had been wholly primitive, direct, and barbaric. Still, whenever Minnie Smellie, flaxen-haired, pink-nosed, and ferret-eyed, indulged in fluent conversation, Rebecca, remembering the old fairy story, could always see toads hopping out of her mouth. It was really very unpleasant, because Minnie could never see them herself; and what was more amazing, Emma Jane perceived nothing of the sort, being almost as blind, too, to the diamonds that fell continually from Rebecca's lips; but Emma Jane's strong point was not her imagination.

A shaky perambulator was found in Mrs. Perkins's wonderful attic; shoes and stockings were furnished by Mrs. Robinson; Miss Jane Sawyer knitted a blanket and some shirts; Thirza Meserve, though too young for an aunt, coaxed from her mother some dresses and nightgowns, and was presented with a green paper certificate allowing her to wheel Jacky up and down the road for an hour under the superintendence of a full Aunt. Each girl, under the constitution of the association, could call Jacky "hers" for two days in the week, and great, though friendly, was the rivalry between them, as they washed, ironed, and sewed for their adored nephew.

19

If Mrs. Cobb had not been the most amiable woman in the world she might have had difficulty in managing the aunts, but she always had Jacky to herself the earlier part of the day and after dusk at night.

Meanwhile Jack-o'-lantern grew healthier and heartier and jollier as the weeks slipped away. Uncle Jerry joined the little company of worshipers and slaves, and one fear alone stirred in all their hearts; not, as a sensible and practical person might imagine, the fear that the recreant father might never return to claim his child, but, on the contrary, that he *might* do so!

October came at length with its cheery days and frosty nights, its glory of crimson leaves and its golden harvest of pumpkins and ripened corn. Rebecca had been down by the Edgewood side of the river and had come up across the pastures for a good-night play with Jacky. Her literary labors had been somewhat interrupted by the joys and responsibilities of vice-motherhood, and the thought book was less frequently drawn from its hiding place under the old haymow in the barn chamber.

Mrs. Cobb stood behind the screen door with her face pressed against the wire netting, and Rebecca could see that she was wiping her eyes.

All at once the child's heart gave one prophetic throb and then stood still. She was like a harp that vibrated with every wind of emotion, whether from another's grief or her own.

She looked down the lane, around the curve of the stone wall, red with woodbine, the lane that would meet the stage road to the station. There, just mounting the crown of the hill and about to disappear on the other side, strode a stranger man, big and tall, with a crop of reddish curly hair showing from under his straw hat. A woman walked by his side, and perched on his shoulder, wearing his most radiant and triumphant mien, as joyous in leaving Edgewood as he had been during every hour of his sojourn there— rode Jack-o'-lantern!

Rebecca gave a cry in which maternal longing and helpless, hopeless jealousy strove for supremacy. Then, with an impetuous movement she started to run after the disappearing trio.

20

Mrs. Cobb opened the door hastily, calling after her, "Rebecca, Rebecca, come back here! You mustn't follow where you haven't any right to go. If there'd been anything to say or do, I'd a' done it."

"He's mine! He's mine!" stormed Rebecca. "At least he's yours and mine!"

"He's his father's first of all," faltered Mrs. Cobb; "don't let's forget that; and we'd ought to be glad and grateful that John Winslow's come to his senses an' remembers he's brought a child into the world and ought to take care of it. Our loss is his gain and it may make a man of him. Come in, and we'll put things away all neat before your Uncle Jerry gets home."

Rebecca sank in a pitiful little heap on Mrs. Cobb's bedroom floor and sobbed her heart out. "Oh, Aunt Sarah, where shall we get another Jack-o'-lantern, and how shall I break it to Emma Jane? What if his father doesn't love him, and what if he forgets to strain the milk or lets him go without his nap? That's the worst of babies that aren't private—you have to part with them sooner or later!"

"Sometimes you have to part with your own, too," said Mrs. Cobb sadly; and though there were lines of sadness in her face there was neither rebellion nor repining, as she folded up the sides of the turn-up bedstead preparatory to banishing it a second time to the attic. "I shall miss Sarah Ellen now more'n ever. Still, Rebecca, we mustn't feel to complain. It's the Lord that giveth and the Lord that taketh away: Blessed be the name of the Lord."

SECOND CHRONICLE

DAUGHTERS OF ZION

I

Abijah Flagg was driving over to Wareham on an errand for old Squire Winship, whose general chore-boy and farmer's assistant he had been for some years.

He passed Emma Jane Perkins's house slowly, as he always did. She was only a little girl of thirteen and he a boy of fifteen or sixteen, but somehow, for no particular reason, he liked to see the sun shine on her thick braids of reddish-brown hair. He admired her china-blue eyes too, and her amiable, friendly expression. He was quite alone in the world, and he always thought that if he had anybody belonging to him he would rather have a sister like Emma Jane Perkins than anything else within the power of Providence to bestow. When she herself suggested this relationship a few years later he cast it aside with scorn, having changed his mind in the interval—but that story belongs to another time and place.

Emma Jane was not to be seen in garden, field, or at the window, and Abijah turned his gaze to the large brick house that came next on the other side of the quiet village street. It might have been closed for a funeral. Neither Miss Miranda nor Miss Jane Sawyer sat at their respective windows knitting, nor was Rebecca Randall's gypsy face to be discerned. Ordinarily that will-o'-the wispish little person could be seen, heard, or felt wherever she was.

"The village must be abed, I guess," mused Abijah, as he neared the Robinsons' yellow cottage, where all the blinds were closed and no sign of life showed on porch or in shed. "No, 't aint, neither," he thought again, as his horse crept cautiously down the hill, for from the direction of the Robinsons' barn chamber there floated out into the air certain burning sentiments set to the tune of

22

"Antioch." The words, to a lad brought up in the orthodox faith, were quite distinguishable:—

"Daugh-ter of Zi-on, from the dust, Ex-alt thy fall-en head!"

Even the most religious youth is stronger on first lines than others, but Abijah pulled up his horse and waited till he caught another familiar verse, beginning:—

"Rebuild thy walls, thy bounds enlarge,
And send thy heralds forth."

"That's Rebecca carrying the air, and I can hear Emma Jane's alto."

"Say to the North, Give up thy charge,

And hold not back, O South, And hold not back, O South," etc.

"Land! ain't they smart, seesawin' up and down in that part they learnt in singin' school! I wonder what they're actin' out, singin' hymn-tunes up in the barn chamber? Some o' Rebecca's doins, I'll be bound! Git dap, Aleck!"

Aleck pursued his serene and steady trot up the hills on the Edgewood side of the river, till at length he approached the green Common where the old Tory Hill meeting-house stood, its white paint and green blinds showing fair and pleasant in the afternoon sun. Both doors were open, and as Abijah turned into the Wareham road the church melodeon pealed out the opening bars of the Missionary Hymn, and presently a score of voices sent the good old tune from the choir-loft out to the dusty road:

"Shall we whose souls are lighted
With Wisdom from on high,
Shall we to men benighted
The lamp of life deny?"

"Land!" exclaimed Abijah under his breath. "They're at it up here, too! That explains it all. There's a missionary meeting at the church, and the girls wa'n't allowed to come so they held one of their own, and I bate ye it's the liveliest of the two."

Abijah Flagg's shrewd Yankee guesses were not far from the truth, though he was not in possession of all the facts. It will be remembered by those who have been in the way of hearing Rebecca's experiences in Riverboro, that the Rev. and Mrs. Burch, returned missionaries from the Far East, together with some of their children, "all born under Syrian skies," as they always explained to interested inquirers, spent a day or two at the brick house, and gave parlor meetings in native costume.

These visitors, coming straight from foreign lands to the little Maine village, brought with them a nameless enchantment to the children, and especially to Rebecca, whose imagination always kindled easily. The romance of that visit had never died in her heart, and among the many careers that dazzled her youthful vision was that of converting such Syrian heathen as might continue in idol worship after the Burches' efforts in their behalf had ceased. She thought at the age of eighteen she might be suitably equipped for storming some minor citadel of Mohammedanism; and Mrs. Burch had encouraged her in the idea, not, it is to be feared, because Rebecca showed any surplus of virtue or Christian grace, but because her gift of language, her tact and sympathy, and her musical talent seemed to fit her for the work.

It chanced that the quarterly meeting of the Maine Missionary Society had been appointed just at the time when a letter from Mrs. Burch to Miss Jane Sawyer suggested that Rebecca should form a children's branch in Riverboro. Mrs. Burch's real idea was that the young people should save their pennies and divert a gentle stream of financial aid into the parent fund, thus learning early in life to be useful in such work, either at home or abroad.

The girls themselves, however, read into her letter no such modest participation in the conversion of the world, and wishing to effect an organization without delay, they chose an afternoon when every house in the village was vacant, and seized upon the Robinsons' barn chamber as the place of meeting.

24

Rebecca, Alice Robinson, Emma Jane Perkins, Candace Milliken, and Persis Watson, each with her hymn book, had climbed the ladder leading to the haymow a half hour before Abijah Flagg had heard the strains of "Daughters of Zion" floating out to the road. Rebecca, being an executive person, had carried, besides her hymn book, a silver call-bell and pencil and paper. An animated discussion regarding one of two names for the society, The Junior Heralds or The Daughters of Zion, had resulted in a unanimous vote for the latter, and Rebecca had been elected president at an early stage of the meeting. She had modestly suggested that Alice Robinson, as the granddaughter of a missionary to China, would be much more eligible.

"No," said Alice, with entire good nature, "whoever is *elected* president, you WILL be, Rebecca—you're that kind—so you might as well have the honor; I'd just as lieves be secretary, anyway."

"If you should want me to be treasurer, I could be, as well as not," said Persis Watson suggestively; "for you know my father keeps china banks at his store—ones that will hold as much as two dollars if you will let them. I think he'd give us one if I happen to be treasurer."

The three principal officers were thus elected at one fell swoop and with an entire absence of that red tape which commonly renders organization so tiresome, Candace Milliken suggesting that perhaps she'd better be vice-president, as Emma Jane Perkins was always so bashful.

"We ought to have more members," she reminded the other girls, "but if we had invited them the first day they'd have all wanted to be officers, especially Minnie Smellie, so it's just as well not to ask them till another time. Is Thirza Meserve too little to join?"

"I can't think why anybody named Meserve should have called a baby Thirza," said Rebecca, somewhat out of order, though the meeting was carried on with small recognition of parliamentary laws. "It always makes me want to say:

She's little, but she's sweet, and absolutely without guile. I think we ought to have her."

"Is 'guile' the same as 'guilt?'" inquired Emma Jane Perkins.

"Yes," the president answered; "exactly the same, except one is written and the other spoken language." (Rebecca was rather good at imbibing information, and a master hand at imparting it!) "Written language is for poems and graduations and occasions like this—kind of like a best Sunday-go-to-meeting dress that you wouldn't like to go blueberrying in for fear of getting it spotted."

"I'd just as 'lieves get 'guile' spotted as not," affirmed the unimaginative Emma Jane. "I think it's an awful foolish word; but now we're all named and our officers elected, what do we do first? It's easy enough for Mary and Martha Burch; they just play at missionarying because their folks work at it, same as Living and I used to make believe be blacksmiths when we were little."

"It must be nicer missionarying in those foreign places," said Persis, "because on 'Afric's shores and India's plains and other spots where Satan reigns' (that's father's favorite hymn) there's always a heathen bowing down to wood and stone. You can take away his idols if he'll let you and give him a bible and the beginning's all made. But who'll we begin on? Jethro Small?"

"Oh, he's entirely too dirty, and foolish besides!" exclaimed Candace. "Why not Ethan Hunt? He swears dreadfully."

"He lives on nuts and is a hermit, and it's a mile to his camp through the thick woods; my mother'll never let me go there," objected Alice. "There's Uncle Tut Judson."

"He's too old; he's most a hundred and deaf as a post," complained Emma Jane. "Besides, his married daughter is a Sabbath-school teacher—why doesn't she teach him to behave? I can't think of anybody just right to start on!"

"Don't talk like that, Emma Jane," and Rebecca's tone had a

26

tinge of reproof in it. "We are a copperated body named the Daughters of Zion, and, of course, we've got to find something to do. Foreigners are the easiest; there's a Scotch family at North Riverboro, an English one in Edgewood, and one Cuban man at Millkin's Mills."

"Haven't foreigners got any religion of their own?" inquired Persis curiously.

"Ye-es, I s'pose so; kind of a one; but foreigners' religions are never right—ours is the only good one." This was from Candace, the deacon's daughter.

"I do think it must be dreadful, being born with a religion and growing up with it, and then finding out it's no use and all your time wasted!" Here Rebecca sighed, chewed a straw, and looked troubled.

"Well, that's your punishment for being a heathen," retorted Candace, who had been brought up strictly.

"But I can't for the life of me see how you can help being a heathen if you're born in Africa," persisted Persis, who was well named.

"You can't." Rebecca was clear on this point. "I had that all out with Mrs. Burch when she was visiting Aunt Miranda. She says they can't help being heathen, but if there's a single mission station in the whole of Africa, they're accountable if they don't go there and get saved."

"Are there plenty of stages and railroads?" asked Alice; "because there must be dreadfully long distances, and what if they couldn't pay the fare?"

"That part of it is so dreadfully puzzly we mustn't talk about it, please," said Rebecca, her sensitive face quivering with the force of the problem. Poor little soul! She did not realize that her superiors in age and intellect had spent many a sleepless night over that same "accountability of the heathen."

"It's too bad the Simpsons have moved away," said Candace. "It's so seldom you can find a real big wicked family like that to save, with only Clara Belle and Susan good in it."

"And numbers count for so much," continued Alice. "My grandmother says if missionaries can't convert about so many in a

27

year the Board advises them to come back to America and take up some other work."

"I know," Rebecca corroborated; "and it's the same with revivalists. At the Centennial picnic at North Riverboro, a revivalist sat opposite to Mr. Ladd and Aunt Jane and me, and he was telling about his wonderful success in Bangor last winter. He'd converted a hundred and thirty in a month, he said, or about four and a third a day. I had just finished fractions, so I asked Mr. Ladd how the third of a man could be converted. He laughed and said it was just the other way; that the man was a third converted. Then he explained that if you were trying to convince a person of his sin on a Monday, and couldn't quite finish by sundown, perhaps you wouldn't want to sit up all night with him, and perhaps he wouldn't want you to; so you'd begin again on Tuesday, and you couldn't say just which day he was converted, because it would be two thirds on Monday and one third on Tuesday."

"Mr. Ladd is always making fun, and the Board couldn't expect any great things of us girls, new beginners," suggested Emma Jane, who was being constantly warned against tautology by her teacher. "I think it's awful rude, anyway, to go right out and try to convert your neighbors; but if you borrow a horse and go to Edgewood Lower Corner, or Milliken's Mills, I s'pose that makes it Foreign Missions."

"Would we each go alone or wait upon them with a committee, as they did when they asked Deacon Tuttle for a contribution for the new hearse?" asked Persis.

"Oh! We must go alone," decided Rebecca; "it would be much more refined and delicate. Aunt Miranda says that one man alone could never get a subscription from Deacon Tuttle, and that's the reason they sent a committee. But it seems to me Mrs. Burch couldn't mean for us to try and convert people when we're none of us even church members, except Candace. I think all we can do is to persuade them to go to meeting and Sabbath school, or give money for the hearse, or the new horse sheds. Now let's all think quietly for a minute or two who's the very most heathenish and reperrehensiblest person in Riverboro."

After a very brief period of silence the words "Jacob Moody" fell from all lips with entire accord.

"You are right," said the president tersely; "and after singing hymn number two hundred seventy four, to be found on the sixty-sixth page, we will take up the question of persuading Mr. Moody to attend divine service or the minister's Bible class, he not having been in the meeting-house for lo! these many years.

'Daughter of Zion, the power that hath saved thee
Extolled with the harp and the timbrel should be.'

"Sing without reading, if you please, omitting the second stanza. Hymn two seventy four, to be found on the sixty-sixth page of the new hymn book or on page thirty two of Emma Jane Perkins's old one."

II

It is doubtful if the Rev. Mr. Burch had ever found in Syria a person more difficult to persuade than the already "gospel-hardened" Jacob Moody of Riverboro.

Tall, gaunt, swarthy, black-bearded—his masses of grizzled, uncombed hair and the red scar across his nose and cheek added to his sinister appearance. His tumble-down house stood on a rocky bit of land back of the Sawyer pasture, and the acres of his farm stretched out on all sides of it. He lived alone, ate alone, plowed, planted, sowed, harvested alone, and was more than willing to die alone, "unwept, unhonored, and unsung." The road that bordered upon his fields was comparatively little used by any one, and notwithstanding the fact that it was thickly set with chokecherry trees and blackberry bushes it had been for years practically deserted by the children. Jacob's Red Astrakhan and Granny Garland trees hung thick with apples, but no Riverboro or Edgewood boy stole them; for terrifying accounts of the fate that had overtaken one urchin in times agone had been handed along

29

from boy to boy, protecting the Moody fruit far better than any police patrol.

Perhaps no circumstances could have extenuated the old man's surly manners or his lack of all citizenly graces and virtues; but his neighbors commonly rebuked his present way of living and forgot the troubled past that had brought it about: the sharp-tongued wife, the unloving and disloyal sons, the daughter's hapless fate, and all the other sorry tricks that fortune had played upon him — at least that was the way in which he had always regarded his disappointments and griefs.

This, then, was the personage whose moral rehabilitation was to be accomplished by the Daughters of Zion. But how?

"Who will volunteer to visit Mr. Moody?" blandly asked the president.

Visit Mr. Moody! It was a wonder the roof of the barn chamber did not fall; it did, indeed echo the words and in some way make them sound more grim and satirical.

"Nobody'll volunteer, Rebecca Rowena Randall, and you know it," said Emma Jane.

"Why don't we draw lots, when none of us wants to speak to him and yet one of us must?"

This suggestion fell from Persis Watson, who had been pale and thoughtful ever since the first mention of Jacob Moody. (She was fond of Granny Garlands; she had once met Jacob; and, as to what befell, well, we all have our secret tragedies!)

"Wouldn't it be wicked to settle it that way?"

"It's gamblers that draw lots."

"People did it in the Bible ever so often."

"It doesn't seem nice for a missionary meeting."

These remarks fell all together upon the president's bewildered ear the while (as she always said in compositions) — "the while" she was trying to adjust the ethics of this unexpected and difficult dilemma.

"It is a very puzzly question," she said thoughtfully. "I could ask Aunt Jane if we had time, but I suppose we haven't. It doesn't seem nice to draw lots, and yet how can we settle it without? We know we mean right, and perhaps it will be. Alice, take this paper and tear off five narrow pieces, all different lengths."

At this moment a voice from a distance floated up to the haymow—a voice saying plaintively: "Will you let me play with you, girls? Huldah has gone to ride, and I'm all alone."

It was the voice of the absolutely-without-guile Thirza Meserve, and it came at an opportune moment.

"If she is going to be a member," said Persis, "why not let her come up and hold the lots? She'd be real honest and not favor anybody."

It seemed an excellent idea, and was followed up so quickly that scarcely three minutes ensued before the guileless one was holding the five scraps in her hot little palm, laboriously changing their places again and again until they looked exactly alike and all rather soiled and wilted.

"Come, girls, draw!" commanded the president. "Thirza, you mustn't chew gum at a missionary meeting, it isn't polite nor holy. Take it out and stick it somewhere till the exercises are over."

The five Daughters of Zion approached the spot so charged with fate, and extended their trembling hands one by one. Then after a moment's silent clutch of their papers they drew nearer to one another and compared them.

Emma Jane Perkins had drawn the short one, becoming thus the destined instrument for Jacob Moody's conversion to a more seemly manner of life!

She looked about her despairingly, as if to seek some painless and respectable method of self-destruction.

"Do let's draw over again," she pleaded. "I'm the worst of all of us. I'm sure to make a mess of it till I kind o' get trained in."

Rebecca's heart sank at this frank confession, which only corroborated her own fears.

"I'm sorry, Emmy, dear," she said, "but our only excuse for drawing lots at all would be to have it sacred. We must think of it as a kind of a sign, almost like God speaking to Moses in the burning bush."

"Oh, I *wish* there was a burning bush right here!" cried the distracted and recalcitrant missionary. "How quick I'd step into it without even stopping to take off my garnet ring!"

"Don't be such a scare-cat, Emma Jane!" exclaimed Candace bracingly. "Jacob Moody can't kill you, even if he has an awful temper. Trot right along now before you get more frightened. Shall we go cross lots with her, Rebecca, and wait at the pasture gate? Then whatever happens Alice can put it down in the minutes of the meeting."

In these terrible crises of life time gallops with such incredible velocity that it seemed to Emma Jane only a breath before she was being dragged through the fields by the other Daughters of Zion, the guileless little Thirza panting in the rear.

At the entrance to the pasture Rebecca gave her an impassioned embrace, and whispering, *"Whatever you do, be careful how you lead up,"* lifted off the top rail and pushed her through the bars. Then the girls turned their backs reluctantly on the pathetic figure, and each sought a tree under whose friendly shade she could watch, and perhaps pray, until the missionary should return from her field of labor.

Alice Robinson, whose compositions were always marked 96 or 97,—100 symbolizing such perfection as could be attained in the mortal world of Riverboro,—Alice, not only Daughter, but Scribe of Zion, sharpened her pencil and wrote a few well-chosen words of introduction, to be used when the records of the afternoon had been made by Emma Jane Perkins and Jacob Moody.

Rebecca's heart beat tumultuously under her gingham dress. She felt that a drama was being enacted, and though unfortunately she was not the central figure, she had at least a modest part in it. The short lot had not fallen to the properest Daughter, that she quite realized; yet would any one of them succeed in winning Jacob Moody's attention, in engaging him in pleasant conversation, and finally in bringing him to a realization of his mistaken way of life? She doubted, but at the same moment her spirits rose at the thought of the difficulties involved in the undertaking.

Difficulties always spurred Rebecca on, but they daunted poor Emma Jane, who had no little thrills of excitement and wonder and fear and longing to sustain her lagging soul. That her interview was to be entered as "minutes" by a secretary seemed to her the last straw. Her blue eyes looked lighter than usual and had the glaze of china saucers; her usually pink cheeks were pale, but she pressed on, determined to be a faithful Daughter of Zion, and above all to be worthy of Rebecca's admiration and respect.

"Rebecca can do anything," she thought, with enthusiastic loyalty, "and I mustn't be any stupider than I can help, or she'll choose one of the other girls for her most intimate friend." So, mustering all her courage, she turned into Jacob Moody's dooryard, where he was chopping wood.

"It's a pleasant afternoon, Mr. Moody," she said in a polite but hoarse whisper, Rebecca's words, *Lead up! Lead up!*" ringing in clarion tones through her brain.

Jacob Moody looked at her curiously. "Good enough, I guess," he growled; "but I don't never have time to look at afternoons."

Emma Jane seated herself timorously on the end of a large log near the chopping block, supposing that Jacob, like other hosts, would pause in his tasks and chat.

"The block is kind of like an idol," she thought; "I wish I could take it away from him, and then perhaps he'd talk."

At this moment Jacob raised his axe and came down on the block with such a stunning blow that Emma Jane fairly leaped into the air.

"You'd better look out, Sissy, or you'll git chips in the eye!" said Moody, grimly going on with his work.

The Daughter of Zion sent up a silent prayer for inspiration, but none came, and she sat silent, giving nervous jumps in spite of herself whenever the axe fell upon the log Jacob was cutting.

Finally, the host became tired of his dumb visitor, and leaning on his axe he said, "Look here, Sis, what have you come for? What's your errant? Do you want apples? Or cider? Or what? Speak out, or GIT out, one or t'other."

Emma Jane, who had wrung her handkerchief into a clammy ball, gave it a last despairing wrench, and faltered: "Wouldn't you like—hadn't you better—don't you think you'd ought to be more constant at meeting and Sabbath school?"

Jacob's axe almost dropped from his nerveless hand, and he regarded the Daughter of Zion with unspeakable rage and disdain. Then, the blood mounting in his face, he gathered himself together, and shouted: "You take yourself off that log and out o' this dooryard double-quick, you imperdent sanct'omus young one! You just let me ketch Bill Perkins' child trying to teach me where I shall go, at my age! Scuttle, I tell ye! And if I see your pious cantin' little mug inside my fence ag'in on sech a business I'll chase ye down the hill or set the dog on ye! *Scoot, I tell ye!*"

Emma Jane obeyed orders summarily, taking herself off the log, out the dooryard, and otherwise scuttling and scooting down the hill at a pace never contemplated even by Jacob Moody, who stood regarding her flying heels with a sardonic grin.

Down she stumbled, the tears coursing over her cheeks and mingling with the dust of her flight; blighted hope, shame, fear, rage, all tearing her bosom in turn, till with a hysterical shriek she fell over the bars and into Rebecca's arms outstretched to receive her. The other Daughters wiped her eyes and supported her almost fainting form, while Thirza, thoroughly frightened, burst into sympathetic tears, and refused to be comforted.

No questions were asked, for it was felt by all parties that Emma Jane's demeanor was answering them before they could be framed.

"He threatened to set the dog on me!" she wailed presently, when, as they neared the Sawyer pasture, she was able to control her voice. "He called me a pious, cantin' young one, and said he'd chase me out o' the dooryard if I ever came again! And he'll tell my father—I know he will, for he hates him like poison."

All at once the adult point of view dawned upon Rebecca. She never saw it until it was too obvious to be ignored. Had they done wrong in interviewing Jacob Moody? Would Aunt Miranda be angry, as well as Mr. Perkins?

"Why was he so dreadful, Emmy?" she questioned tenderly. "What did you say first? How did you lead up to it?"

Emma Jane sobbed more convulsively, and wiped her nose and eyes impartially as she tried to think.

"I guess I never led up at all; not a mite. I didn't know what

34

you meant. I was sent on an errant, and I went and done it the best I could! (Emma Jane's grammar always lapsed in moments of excitement.) And then Jake roared at me like Squire Winship's bull.... And he called my face a mug.... You shut up that secretary book, Alice Robinson! If you write down a single word I'll never speak to you again.... And I don't want to be a member' another minute for fear of drawing another short lot. I've got enough of the Daughters or Zion to last me the rest o' my life! I don't care who goes to meetin' and who don't."

The girls were at the Perkins's gate by this time, and Emma Jane went sadly into the empty house to remove all traces of the tragedy from her person before her mother should come home from the church.

The others wended their way slowly down the street, feeling that their promising missionary branch had died almost as soon as it had budded.

"Goodby," said Rebecca, swallowing lumps of disappointment and chagrin as she saw the whole inspiring plan break and vanish into thin air like an iridescent bubble. "It's all over and we won't ever try it again. I'm going in to do overcasting as hard as I can, because I hate that the worst. Aunt Jane must write to Mrs. Burch that we don't want to be home missionaries. Perhaps we're not big enough, anyway. I'm perfectly certain it's nicer to convert people when they're yellow or brown or any color but white; and I believe it must be easier to save their souls than it is to make them go to meeting."

THIRD CHRONICLE

REBECCA'S THOUGHT BOOK

I

The "Sawyer girls'" barn still had its haymow in Rebecca's time, although the hay was a dozen years old or more, and, in the opinion of the occasional visiting horse, sadly juiceless and wanting in flavor. It still sheltered, too, old Deacon Israel Sawyer's carryall and mowing-machine, with his pung, his sleigh, and a dozen other survivals of an earlier era, when the broad acres of the brick house went to make one of the finest farms in Riverboro.

There were no horses or cows in the stalls nowadays; no pig grunting comfortably of future spare ribs in the sty; no hens to peck the plants in the cherished garden patch. The Sawyer girls were getting on in years, and, mindful that care once killed a cat, they ordered their lives with the view of escaping that particular doom, at least, and succeeded fairly well until Rebecca's advent made existence a trifle more sensational.

Once a month for years upon years, Miss Miranda and Miss Jane had put towels over their heads and made a solemn visit to the barn, taking off the enameled cloth coverings (occasionally called "emmanuel covers" in Riverboro), dusting the ancient implements, and sometimes sweeping the heaviest of the cobwebs from the corners, or giving a brush to the floor.

Deacon Israel's tottering ladder still stood in its accustomed place, propped against the haymow, and the heavenly stairway leading to eternal glory scarcely looked fairer to Jacob of old than this to Rebecca. By means of its dusty rounds she mounted, mounted, mounted far away from time and care and maiden aunts, far away from childish tasks and childish troubles, to the barn chamber, a place so full of golden dreams, happy reveries, and vague longings, that, as her little brown hands clung to the sides of the ladder and her feet trod the rounds cautiously in her ascent, her heart almost stopped beating in the sheer joy of anticipation.

Once having gained the heights, the next thing was to unlatch the heavy doors and give them a gentle swing outward. Then, oh, ever new Paradise! Then, oh, ever lovely green and growing world! For Rebecca had that something in her soul that

> "Gives to seas and sunset skies
> The unspent beauty of surprise."

At the top of Guide Board hill she could see Alice Robinson's barn with its shining weather vane, a huge burnished fish that swam with the wind and foretold the day to all Riverboro. The meadow, with its sunny slopes stretching up to the pine woods, was sometimes a flowing sheet of shimmering grass, sometimes—when daisies and buttercups were blooming—a vision of white and gold. Sometimes the shorn stubble would be dotted with "the happy hills of hay," and a little later the rock maple on the edge of the pines would stand out like a golden ball against the green; its neighbor, the sugar maple, glowing beside it, brave in scarlet.

It was on one of these autumn days with a wintry nip in the air that Adam Ladd (Rebecca's favorite "Mr. Aladdin"), after searching for her in field and garden, suddenly noticed the open doors of the barn chamber, and called to her. At the sound of his vice she dropped her precious diary, and flew to the edge of the haymow. He never forgot the vision of the startled little poetess, book in one mittened hand, pencil in the other, dark hair all ruffled, with the picturesque addition of an occasional glade of straw, her cheeks crimson, her eyes shining.

"A Sappho in mittens!" he cried laughingly, and at her eager question told her to look up the unknown lady in the school encyclopedia, when she was admitted to the Female Seminary at Wareham.

Now, all being ready, Rebecca went to a corner of the haymow, and withdrew a thick blank-book with mottled covers. Out of her gingham apron pocket came a pencil, a bit of rubber, and some

37

pieces of brown paper; then she seated herself gravely on the floor, and drew an inverted soapbox nearer to her for a table.

The book was reverently opened, and there was a serious reading of the extracts already carefully copied therein. Most of them were apparently to the writer's liking, for dimples of pleasure showed themselves now and then, and smiles of obvious delight played about her face; but once in a while there was a knitting of the brows and a sigh of discouragement, showing that the artist in the child was not wholly satisfied.

Then came the crucial moment when the budding author was supposedly to be racked with the throes of composition; but seemingly there were no throes. Other girls could wield the darning or crochet or knitting needle, and send the tatting shuttle through loops of the finest cotton; hemstitch, oversew, braid hair in thirteen strands, but the pencil was never obedient in their fingers, and the pen and ink-pot were a horror from early childhood to the end of time.

Not so with Rebecca; her pencil moved as easily as her tongue, and no more striking simile could possibly be used. Her handwriting was not Spencerian; she had neither time, nor patience, it is to be feared, for copybook methods, and her unformed characters were frequently the despair of her teachers; but write she could, write she would, write she must and did, in season and out; from the time she made pothooks at six, till now, writing was the easiest of all possible tasks; to be indulged in as solace and balm when the terrors of examples in least common multiple threatened to dethrone the reason, or the rules of grammar loomed huge and unconquerable in the near horizon.

As to spelling, it came to her in the main by free grace, and not by training, and though she slipped at times from the beaten path, her extraordinary ear and good visual memory kept her from many or flagrant mistakes. It was her intention, especially when saying her prayers at night, to look up all doubtful words in her small dictionary, before copying her Thoughts into the sacred book for the inspiration of posterity; but when genius burned with a brilliant flame, and particularly when she was in the barn and the dictionary in the house, impulse as usual carried the day.

38

There sits Rebecca, then, in the open door of the Sawyers barn chamber—the sunset door. How many a time had her grandfather, the good deacon, sat just underneath in his tipped-back chair, when Mrs. Israel's temper was uncertain, and the serenity of the barn was in comforting contrast to his own fireside!

The open doors swinging out to the peaceful landscape, the solace of the pipe, not allowed in the "settin'-room"—how beautifully these simple agents have ministered to the family peace in days agone! "If I hadn't had my barn and my store *both*, I couldn't never have lived in holy matrimony with Maryliza!" once said Mr. Watson feelingly.

But the deacon, looking on his waving grass fields, his tasseling corn and his timber lands, bright and honest as were his eyes, never saw such visions as Rebecca. The child, transplanted from her home farm at Sunnybrook, from the care of the overworked but easy-going mother, and the companionship of the scantily fed, scantily clothed, happy-go-lucky brothers and sisters—she had indeed fallen on shady days in Riverboro. The blinds were closed in every room of the house but two, and the same might have been said of Miss Miranda's mind and heart, though Miss Jane had a few windows opening to the sun, and Rebecca already had her unconscious hand on several others. Brickhouse rules were rigid and many for a little creature so full of life, but Rebecca's gay spirit could not be pinioned in a strait jacket for long at a time; it escaped somehow and winged its merry way into the sunshine and free air; if she were not allowed to sing in the orchard, like the wild bird she was, she could still sing in the cage, like the canary.

II

If you had opened the carefully guarded volume with the mottled covers, you would first have seen a wonderful title page, constructed apparently on the same lines as an obituary, or the inscription on a tombstone, save for the quantity and variety of information contained in it. Much of the matter would seem to the captious critic better adapted to the body of the book than to the title page, but Rebecca was apparently anxious that the principal personages in her chronicle should be well described at the outset.

She seems to have had a conviction that heredity plays its part in the evolution of genius, and her belief that the world will be inspired by the possession of her Thoughts is too artless to be offensive. She evidently has respect for rich material confided to her teacher, and one can imagine Miss Dearborn's woe had she been confronted by Rebecca's chosen literary executor and bidden to deliver certain "Valuable Poetry and Thoughts," the property of posterity "unless carelessly destroyed."

THOUGHT BOOK
of
REBECCA ROWENA RANDALL

Really of
Sunnybrook Farm
But temporily of
The Brick House Riverboro.
Own niece of Miss Miranda and Jane Sawyer
Second of seven children of her father, Mr. L. D. M. Randall (Now at rest
in Temperance cemmetary and there will be a monument as soon as we
pay off the mortgage on the farm)
Also of her mother Mrs. Aurelia Randall

In case of Death the best of these Thoughts
May be printed in my Remerniscences
For the Sunday School Library at Temperance, Maine
Which needs more books fearfully
And I hereby Will and Testament them
To Mr. Adam Ladd
Who bought 300 cakes of soap from me
And thus secured a premium
A Greatly Needed Banquet Lamp
For my friends the Simpsons.

He is the only one that incourages
My writing Remerniscences and
My teacher Miss Dearborn will
Have much valuable Poetry and Thoughts
To give him unless carelessly destroyed.

The pictures are by the same hand that
Wrote the Thoughts.

It is not now decided whether Rebecca Rowena Randall will be a painter or an author, but after her death it will be known which she has been, if any.

FINIS

From the title page, with its wealth of detail, and its unnecessary and irrelevant information, the book ripples on like a brook, and to the weary reader of problem novels it may have something of the brook's refreshing quality.

OUR DIARIES

May, 187—

All the girls are keeping a diary because Miss Dearborn was very much ashamed when the school trustees told her that most of the girls' and all of the boys' compositions were disgraceful, and must be improved upon next term. She asked the boys to write letters to her once a week instead of keeping a diary, which they thought was girlish like playing with dolls. The boys thought it was dreadful to have to write letters every seven days, but she told them it was not half as bad for them as it was for her who had to read them.

To make my diary a little different I am going to call it a Thought Book (written just like that, with capitals). I have thoughts that I never can use unless I write them down, for Aunt Miranda

41

always says, Keep your thoughts to yourself. Aunt Jane lets me tell her some, but does not like my queer ones and my true thoughts are mostly queer. Emma Jane does not mind hearing them now and then, and that is my only chance.

If Miss Dearborn does not like the name Thought Book I will call it Remerniscences (written just like that with a capital R). Remerniscences are things you remember about yourself and write down in case you should die. Aunt Jane doesn't like to read any other kind of books but just lives of interesting dead people and she says that is what Longfellow (who was born in the state of Maine and we should be very proud of it and try to write like him) meant in his poem:

"Lives of great men all remind us
We should make our lives sublime,
And departing, leave behind us
Footprints on the sands of time."

I know what this means because when Emma Jane and I went to the beach with Uncle Jerry Cobb we ran along the wet sand and looked at the shapes our boots made, just as if they were stamped in wax. Emma Jane turns in her left foot (splayfoot the boys call it, which is not polite) and Seth Strout had just patched one of my shoes and it all came out in the sand pictures. When I learned The Psalm of Life for Friday afternoon speaking I thought I shouldn't like to leave a patched footprint, nor have Emma Jane's look crooked on the sands of time, and right away I thought Oh! What a splendid thought for my Thought Book when Aunt Jane buys me a fifteen-cent one over to Watson's store.

. . . .

June, 187—

I told Aunt Jane I was going to begin my Remerniscences, and she says I am full young, but I reminded her that Candace Milliken's sister died when she was ten, leaving no footprints whatever, and if I should die suddenly who would write down my Remerniscences? Aunt Miranda says the sun and moon would rise and set just the same, and it was no matter if they didn't get written down, and to go up attic and find her piece-bag; but I said it would, as there was only one of everybody in the world, and nobody else could do their remerniscensing for them. If I should die tonight I know now who would describe me right. Miss Dearborn would say one thing and brother John another. Emma Jane would try to do me justice, but has no words; and I am glad Aunt Miranda never takes the pen in hand.

My dictionary is so small it has not many genteel words in it, and I cannot find how to spell Remerniscences, but I remember from the cover of Aunt Jane's book that there was an "s" and a "c" close together in the middle of it, which I thought foolish and not needful.

All the girls like their dairies very much, but Minnie Smellie got Alice Robinson's where she had hid it under the school wood pile and read it all through. She said it was no worse than reading anybody's composition, but we told her it was just like peeking through a keyhole, or listening at a window, or opening a bureau drawer. She said she didn't look at it that way, and I told her that unless her eyes got unscealed she would never leave any kind of a sublime footprint on the sands of time. I told her a diary was very sacred as you generally poured your deepest feelings into it expecting nobody to look at it but yourself and your indulgent heavenly Father who seeeth all things.

Of course it would not hurt Persis Watson to show her diary because she has not a sacred plan and this is the way it goes, for she reads it out loud to us:

"Arose at six this morning—(you always arise in a diary but

you say get up when you talk about it). Ate breakfast at half past six. Had soda biscuits, coffee, fish hash and doughnuts. Wiped the dishes, fed the hens and made my bed before school. Had a good arithmetic lesson, but went down two in spelling. At half past four played hide and coop in the Sawyer pasture. Fed hens and went to bed at eight."

She says she can't put in what doesn't happen, but as I don't think her diary is interesting she will ask her mother to have meat hash instead of fish, with pie when the doughnuts give out, and she will feed the hens before breakfast to make a change. We are all going now to try and make something happen every single day so the diaries won't be so dull and the footprints so common.

. . . .

AN UNCOMMON THOUGHT

July 187—

We dug up our rosecakes today, and that gave me a good Remerniscence. The way you make rose cakes is, you take the leaves of full blown roses and mix them with a little cinnamon and as much brown sugar as they will give you, which is never half enough except Persis Watson, whose affectionate parents let her go to the barrel in their store. Then you do up little bits like sedlitz powders, first in soft paper and then in brown, and bury them in the ground and let them stay as long as you possibly can hold out; then dig them up and eat them. Emma Jane and I stick up little signs over the holes in the ground with the date we buried them and when they'll be done enough to dig up, but we can never wait. When Aunt Jane saw us she said it was the first thing for children to learn,—not to be impatient,—so when I went to the barn chamber I made a poem.

44

IMPATIENCE

We dug our rose cakes up oh! all too soon.
T was in the orchard just at noon.
T was in a bright July forenoon.
T was in the sunny afternoon.
T was underneath the harvest moon.

It was not that way at all; it was a foggy morning before school, and I should think poets could never possibly get to heaven, for it is so hard to stick to the truth when you are writing poetry. Emma Jane thinks it is nobody's business when we dug the rosecakes up. I like the line about the harvest moon best, but it would give a wrong idea of our lives and characters to the people that read my Thoughts, for they would think we were up late nights, so I have fixed it like this:

IMPATIENCE

We dug our rose cakes up oh! all too soon,
We thought their sweetness would be such a boon.
We ne'er suspicioned they would not be done
After three days of autumn wind and sun.
Why did we from the earth our treasures draw?
Twas not for fear that rat or mole might naw,
An aged aunt doth say impatience was the reason,
She says that youth is ever out of season.

That is just as Aunt Jane said it, and it gave me the thought for the poem which is rather uncommon.

. . . .

A DREADFUL QUESTION

September, 187—

Which has been the most benefercent influence on Character—
Punishment or Reward?

This truly dreadful question was given us by Dr. Moses when
he visited school today. He is a School Committee; not a whole one
but I do not know the singular number of him. He told us we could
ask our families what they thought, though he would rather we
wouldn't, but we must write our own words and he would hear
them next week.

After he went out and shut the door the scholars were all
plunged in gloom and you could have heard a pin drop. Alice
Robinson cried and borrowed my handkerchief, and the boys
looked as if the schoolhouse had been struck by lightning. The
worst of all was poor Miss Dearborn, who will lose her place if she
does not make us better scholars soon, for Dr. Moses has a daughter
all ready to put right in to the school and she can board at home
and save all her wages. Libby Moses is her name.

Miss Dearborn stared out the window, and her mouth and chin
shook like Alice Robinson's, for she knew, ah! all to well, what the
coming week would bring forth.

Then I raised my hand for permission to speak, and stood up
and said: "Miss Dearborn, don't you mind! Just explain to us what
benefercent' means and we'll write something real interesting; for
all of us know what punishment is, and have seen others get
rewards, and it is not so bad a subject as some." And Dick Carter
whispered, *"Good on your head, Rebecca!"* which mean he was sorry
for her too, and would try his best, but has no words.

Then teacher smiled and said benefercent meant good or
healthy for anybody, and would all rise who thought punishment
made the best scholars and men and women; and everybody sat
stock still.

And then she asked all to stand who believed that rewards
produced the finest results, and there was a mighty sound like unto

the rushing of waters, but really was our feet scraping the floor, and the scholars stood up, and it looked like an army, though it was only nineteen, because of the strong belief that was in them. Then Miss Dearborn laughed and said she was thankful for every whipping she had when she was a child, and Living Perkins said perhaps we hadn't got to the thankful age, or perhaps her father hadn't used a strap, and she said oh! no, it was her mother with the open hand; and Dick Carter said he wouldn't call that punishment, and Sam Simpson said so too.

I am going to write about the subject in my Thought Book first, and when I make it into a composition, I can leave out anything about the family or not genteel, as there is much to relate about punishment not pleasant or nice and hardly polite.

. . . .

PUNISHMENT

Punishment is a very puzzly thing, but I believe in it when really deserved, only when I punish myself it does not always turn out well. When I leaned over the new bridge, and got my dress all paint, and Aunt Sarah Cobb couldn't get it out, I had to wear it spotted for six months which hurt my pride, but was right. I stayed at home from Alice Robinson's birthday party for a punishment, and went to the circus next day instead, but Alice's parties are very cold and stiff, as Mrs. Robinson makes the boys stand on newspapers if they come inside the door, and the blinds are always shut, and Mrs. Robinson tells me how bad her liver complaint is this year. So I thought, to pay for the circus and a few other things, I ought to get more punishment, and I threw my pink parasol down the well, as the mothers in the missionary books throw their infants to the crocodiles in the Ganges river. But it got stuck in the chain that holds the bucket, and Aunt Miranda had to get Abijah Flagg to take out all the broken bits before we could ring up water.

I punished myself this way because Aunt Miranda said that unless I improved I would be nothing but a Burden and a Blight.

47

There was an old man used to go by our farm carrying a lot of broken chairs to bottom, and mother used to say—"Poor man! His back is too weak for such a burden!" and I used to take him out a doughnut, and this is the part I want to go into the Remerniscences. Once I told him we were sorry the chairs were so heavy, and he said *they didn't seem so heavy when he had et the doughnut*. This does not mean that the doughnut was heavier than the chairs which is what brother John said, but it is a beautiful thought and shows how the human race should have sympathy, and help bear burdens.

I know about a Blight, for there was a dreadful east wind over at our farm that destroyed all the little young crops just out of the ground, and the farmers called it the Blight. And I would rather be hail, sleet, frost, or snow than a Blight, which is mean and secret, and which is the reason I threw away the dearest thing on earth to me, the pink parasol that Miss Ross brought me from Paris, France. I have also wrapped up my bead purse in three papers and put it away marked not to be opened till after my death unless needed for a party.

I must not be Burden, I must not be Blight,
The angels in heaven would weep at the sight.

. . . .

REWARDS

A good way to find out which has the most benefercent effect would be to try rewards on myself this next week and write my composition the very last day, when I see how my character is. It is hard to find rewards for yourself, but perhaps Aunt Jane and some of the girls would each give me one to help out. I could carry my bead purse to school every day, or wear my coral chain a little while before I go to sleep at night. I could read Cora or the Sorrows of a Doctor's Wife a little oftener, but that's all the rewards I can think of. I fear Aunt Miranda would say they are wicked but oh! if they should turn out benefercent how glad and joyful life would be to me! A sweet and beautiful character, beloved by my teacher and schoolmates, admired and petted by my aunts and neighbors, yet carrying my bead purse constantly, with perhaps my best hat on Wednesday afternoons, as well as Sundays!

. . . .

A GREAT SHOCK

The reason why Alice Robinson could not play was, she was being punished for breaking her mother's blue platter. Just before supper my story being finished I went up Guide Board hill to see how she was bearing up and she spoke to me from her window. She said she did not mind being punished because she hadn't been for a long time, and she hoped it would help her with her composition. She thought it would give her thoughts, and tomorrow's the last day for her to have any. This gave me a good idea and I told her to call her father up and beg him to beat her violently. It would hurt, I said, but perhaps none of the other girls would have a punishment like that, and her composition would be all different and splendid. I would borrow Aunt Miranda's witchhayzel and pour it on her wounds like the Samaritan in the Bible.

I went up again after supper with Dick Carter to see how it turned out. Alice came to the window and Dick threw up a note tied to a stick. I had written: *"Demand your punishment to the full. be brave like Dolores' mother in the* Martyrs of Spain.*"*

She threw down an answer, and it was: *"you just be like Dolores' mother yourself if you're so smart!"* Then she stamped away from the window and my feelings were hurt, but Dick said perhaps she was hungry, and that made her cross. And as Dick and I turned to go out of the yard we looked back and I saw something I can never forget. (The Great Shock) Mrs. Robinson was out behind the barn feeding the turkies. Mr. Robinson came softly out of the side door in the orchard and looking everywheres around he stepped to the wire closet and took out a saucer of cold beans with a pickled beet

49

on top, and a big piece of blueberry pie. Then he crept up the back stairs and we could see Alice open her door and take in the supper.

Oh! What will become of her composition, and how can she tell anything of the benefercent effects of punishment, when she is locked up by one parent, and fed by the other? I have forgiven her for the way she snapped me up for, of course, you couldn't beg your father to beat you when he was bringing you blueberry pie. Mrs. Robinson makes a kind that leaks out a thick purple juice into the plate and needs a spoon and blacks your mouth, but is heavenly.

. . . .

A DREAM

The week is almost up and very soon Dr. Moses will drive up to the school house like Elijah in the chariot and come in to hear us read. There is a good deal of sickness among us. Some of the boys are not able to come to school just now, but hope to be about again by Monday, when Dr. Moses goes away to a convention. It is a very hard composition to write, somehow. Last night I dreamed that the river was ink and I kept dipping into it and writing with a penstalk made of a young pine tree. I sliced great slabs of marble off the side of one of the White Mountains, the one you see when going to meeting, and wrote on those. Then I threw them all into the falls, not being good enough for Dr. Moses.

Dick Carter had a splendid boy to stay over Sunday. He makes the real newspaper named The Pilot published by the boys at Wareham Academy. He says when he talks about himself in writing he calls himself "we," and it sounds much more like print, besides conscealing him more.

Example: Our hair was measured this morning and has grown two inches since last time.... We have a loose tooth that troubles us very much... Our inkspot that we made by negligence on our only white petticoat we have been able to remove with lemon and milk. Some of our petticoat came out with the spot.

I shall try it in my composition sometime, for of course I shall write for the Pilot when I go to Wareham Seminary. Uncle Jerry Cobb says that I shall, and thinks that in four years I might rise to be editor if they ever have girls.

I have never been more good than since I have been rewarding myself steady, even to asking Aunt Miranda kindly to offer me a company jelly tart, not because I was hungry, but for an experement I was trying, and would explain to her sometime.

She said she never thought it was wise to experement with your stomach, and I said, with a queer thrilling look, it was not my stomach but my soul, that was being tried. Then she gave me the tart and walked away all puzzled and nervous.

The new minister has asked me to come and see him any Saturday afternoon as he writes poetry himself, but I would rather not ask him about this composition.

Ministers never believe in rewards, and it is useless to hope that they will. We had the wrath of God four times in sermons this last summer, but God cannot be angry all the time,—nobody could, especially in summer; Mr. Baxter is different and calls his wife dear which is lovely and the first time I ever heard it in Riverboro. Mrs. Baxter is another kind of people too, from those that live in Temperance. I like to watch her in meeting and see her listen to her husband who is young and handsome for a minister; it gives me very queer and uncommon feelings, when they look at each other, which they always do when not otherwise engaged.

She has different clothes from anybody else. Aunt Miranda says you must think only of two things: will your dress keep you warm and will it wear well and there is nobody in the world to know how I love pink and red and how I hate drab and green and how I never wear my hat with the black and yellow porkupine quills without wishing it would blow into the river.

> Whene'er I take my walks abroad
> How many quills I see.
> But as they are not porkupines
> They never come to me.

51

COMPOSITION

Which has the most Benefercent Effect on the Character, Punishment or Reward?
by
Rebecca Rowena Randall
(This copy not corrected by Miss Dearborn yet.)

We find ourselves very puzzled in approaching this truly great and national question though we have tried very ernestly to understand it, so as to show how wisely and wonderfully our dear teacher guides the youthful mind, it being her wish that our composition class shall long be remembered in Riverboro Centre.

We would say first of all that punishment seems more benefercently needed by boys than girls. Boys' sins are very violent, like stealing fruit, profane language, playing truant, fighting, breaking windows, and killing innocent little flies and bugs. If these were not taken out of them early in life it would be impossible for them to become like our martyred president, Abraham Lincoln.

Although we have asked everybody on our street, they think boys' sins can only be whipped out of them with a switch or strap, which makes us feel very sad, as boys when not sinning the dreadful sins mentioned above seem just as good as girls, and never cry when switched, and say it does not hurt much.

We now approach girls, which we know better, being one. Girls seem better than boys because their sins are not so noisy and showy. They can disobey their parents and aunts, whisper in silent hour, cheat in lessons, say angry things to their schoolmates, tell lies, be sulky and lazy, but all these can be conducted quite ladylike and genteel, and nobody wants to strap girls because their skins are tender and get black and blue very easily.

Punishments make one very unhappy and rewards very happy, and one would think when one is happy one would behave the best. We were acquainted with a girl who gave herself rewards every day for a week, and it seemed to make her as lovely a character as one could wish; but perhaps if one went on for years giving rewards to onesself one would become selfish. One cannot tell, one can only fear.

If a dog kills a sheep we should whip him straight away, and on the very spot where he can see the sheep, or he will not know what we mean, and may forget and kill another. The same is true of the human race. We must be firm and patient in punishing, no matter how much we love the one who has done wrong, and how hungry she is. It does no good to whip a person with one hand and offer her a pickled beet with the other. This confuses her mind, and she may grow up not knowing right from wrong.[1]

We now respectfully approach the Holy Bible and the people in the Bible were punished the whole time, and that would seem to make it right. Everybody says Whom the Lord loveth he chasteneth; but we think ourself, that the Lord is a better punisher than we are, and knows better how and when to do it having attended to it ever since the year B.C. while the human race could not know about it till 1492 A.D., which is when Columbus discovered America.

We do not believe we can find out all about this truly great and national subject till we get to heaven, where the human race, strapped and unstrapped, if any, can meet together and laying down their harps discuss how they got there.

And we would gently advise boys to be more quiet and genteel in conduct and try rewards to see how they would work. Rewards are not all like the little rosebud merit cards we receive on Fridays, and which boys sometimes tear up and fling scornfully to the breeze when they get outside, but girls preserve carefully in an envelope.

Some rewards are great and glorious, for boys can get to be governor or school trustee or road commissioner or president, while girls can only be wife and mother. But all of us can have the ornament of a meek and lowly spirit, especially girls, who have more use for it than boys.

R. R. R.

---

[1] The striking example of the pickled beet was removed from the essay by the refined but ruthless Miss Dearborn, who strove patiently, but vainly, to keep such vulgar images out of her pupils' literary efforts.

53

October, 187—

There are people in books and people in Riverboro, and they are not the same kind. They never talk of chargers and palfreys in the village, nor say How oft and Methinks, and if a Scotchman out of Rob Roy should come to Riverboro and want to marry one of us girls we could not understand him unless he made motions; though Huldah Meserve says if a nobleman of high degree should ask her to be his,—one of vast estates with serfs at his bidding,—she would be able to guess his meaning in any language.

Uncle Jerry Cobb thinks that Riverboro people would not make a story, but I know that some of them would.

Jack-o'-lantern, though only a baby, was just like a real story if anybody had written a piece about him: How his mother was dead and his father ran away and Emma Jane and I got Aunt Sarah Cobb to keep him so Mr. Perkins wouldn't take him to the poor farm; and about our lovely times with him that summer, and our dreadful loss when his father remembered him in the fall and came to take him away; and how Aunt Sarah carried the trundle bed up attic again and Emma Jane and I heard her crying and stole away.

Mrs. Peter Meserve says Grandpa Sawyer was a wonderful hand at stories before his spirit was broken by grandmother. She says he was the life of the store and tavern when he was a young man, though generally sober, and she thinks I take after him, because I like compositions better than all the other lessons; but mother says I take after father, who always could say everything nicely whether he had anything to say or not; so methinks I should be grateful to both of them. They are what is called ancestors and much depends upon whether you have them or not. The Simpsons have not any at all. Aunt Miranda says the reason everybody is so prosperous around here is because their ancestors were all first settlers and raised on burnt ground. This should make us very proud.

Methinks and methought are splendid words for compositions. Miss Dearborn likes them very much, but Alice and I never bring

54

them in to suit her. Methought means the same as I thought, but sounds better. Example: If you are telling a dream you had about your aged aunt:

> *Methought I heard her say*
> *My child you have so useful been*
> *You need not sew to-day.*

This is a good example one way, but too unlikely, woe is me!

This afternoon I was walking over to the store to buy molasses, and as I came off the bridge and turned up the hill, I saw lots and lots of heelprints in the side of the road, heelprints with little spike holes in them.

"Oh! The river drivers have come from up country," I thought, "and they'll be breaking the jam at our falls tomorrow." I looked everywhere about and not a man did I see, but still I knew I was not mistaken for the heelprints could not lie. All the way over and back I thought about it, though unfortunately forgetting the molasses, and Alice Robinson not being able to come out, I took playtime to write a story. It is the first grown-up one I ever did, and is intended to be like Cora the Doctor's Wife, not like a school composition. It is written for Mr. Adam Ladd, and people like him who live in Boston, and is the printed kind you get money for, to pay off a mortgage.

LANCELOT OR THE PARTED LOVERS

A beautiful village maiden was betrothed to a stallwart river driver, but they had high and bitter words and parted, he to weep into the crystal stream as he drove his logs, and she to sigh and moan as she went about her round of household tasks.

At eventide the maiden was wont to lean over the bridge and her tears also fell into the foaming stream; so, though the two unhappy lovers did not know it, the river was their friend, the only one to whom they told their secrets and wept into.

The months crept on and it was the next July when the maiden was passing over the bridge and up the hill. Suddenly she spied footprints on the sands of time.

"The river drivers have come again!" she cried, putting her hand to her side for she had a slight heart trouble like Cora and Mrs. Peter Meserve, that doesn't kill.

"They *have* come indeed; *especially one you know*," said a voice, and out from the alder bushes sprung Lancelot Littlefield, for that was the lover's name and it was none other than he. His hair was curly and like living gold. His shirt, white of flannel, was new and dry, and of a handsome color, and as the maiden looked at him she could think of nought but a fairy prince.

"Forgive," she mermered, stretching out her waisted hands.

"Nay, sweet," he replied. "'Tis I should say that to you," and bending gracefully on one knee he kissed the hem of her dress. It was a rich pink gingham check, ellaborately ornamented with white tape trimming.

Clasping each other to the heart like Cora and the Doctor, they stood there for a long while, till they heard the rumble of wheels on the bridge and knew they must disentangle.

The wheels came nearer and verily! it was the maiden's father.

"Can I wed with your fair daughter this very moon," asked Lancelot, who will not be called his whole name again in this story.

"You may," said the father, "for lo! she has been ready and waiting for many months." This he said not noting how he was shaming the maiden, whose name was Linda Rowenetta.

Then and there the nuptial day was appointed and when it came, the marriage knot was tied upon the river bank where first they met; the river bank where they had parted in anger, and where they had again scealeld their vows and clasped each other to the heart. And it was very low water that summer, and the river always thought it was because no tears dropped into it but so many smiles that like sunshine they dried it up.

R. R. R.

FINIS

56

CAREERS

Long ago when I used to watch Miss Ross painting the old mill at Sunnybrook I thought I would be a painter, for Miss Ross went to Paris France where she bought my bead purse and pink parasol and I thought I would like to see a street with beautiful bright-colored things sparkling and hanging in the store windows.

Then when the missionaries from Syria came to stay at the brick house Mrs. Burch said that after I had experienced religion I must learn music and train my voice and go out to heathen lands and save souls, so I thought that would be my career. But we girls tried to have a branch and be home missionaries and it did not work well. Emma Jane's father would not let her have her birthday party when he found out what she had done and Aunt Jane sent me up to Jake Moody's to tell him we did not mean to be rude when we asked him to go to meeting more often. He said all right, but just let him catch that little dough-faced Perkins young one in his yard once more and she'd have reason to remember the call, which was just as rude and impolite as our trying to lead him to a purer and a better life.

Then Uncle Jerry and Mr. Aladdin and Miss Dearborn liked my compositions, and I thought I'd better be a writer, for I must be something the minute I'm seventeen, or how shall we ever get the mortgage off the farm? But even that hope is taken away from me now, for Uncle Jerry made fun of my story Lancelot Or The Parted Lovers and I have decided to be a teacher like Miss Dearborn.

The pathetic announcement of a change in the career and life purposes of Rebecca was brought about by her reading the grown-up story to Mr. and Mrs. Jeremiah Cobb after supper in the orchard. Uncle Jerry was the person who had maintained all along that Riverboro people would not make a story; and Lancelot or The Parted Lovers was intended to refute that assertion at once and forever; an assertion which Rebecca regarded (quite truly) as untenable, though why she certainly never could have explained. Unfortunately Lancelot was a poor missionary, quite unfitted for

57

the high achievements to which he was destined by the youthful novelist, and Uncle Jerry, though a stage-driver and no reading man, at once perceived the flabbiness and transparency of the Parted Lovers the moment they were held up to his inspection.

"You see Riverboro people WILL make a story!" asserted Rebecca triumphantly as she finished her reading and folded the paper. "And it all came from my noticing the river drivers' tracks by the roadside, and wondering about them; and wondering always makes stories; the minister says so."

"Ye-es," allowed Uncle Jerry reflectively, tipping his chair back against the apple tree and forcing his slow mind to violent and instantaneous action, for Rebecca was his pride and joy; a person, in his opinion, of superhuman talent, one therefore to be "whittled into shape" if occasion demanded.

"It's a Riverboro story, sure enough, because you've got the river and the bridge and the hill and the drivers all right there in it; but there's something awful queer bout it; the folks don't act Riverboro, and don't talk Riverboro, cordin' to my notions. I call it a reg'lar book story."

"But," objected Rebecca, "the people in Cinderella didn't act like us, and you thought that was a beautiful story when I told it to you."

"I know," replied Uncle Jerry, gaining eloquence in the heat of argument. "They didn't act like us, but 't any rate they acted like 'emselves! Somehow they was all of a piece. Cinderella was a little too good, mebbe, and the sisters was most too thunderin' bad to live on the face o' the earth, and that fayry old lady that kep' the punkin' coach up her sleeve—well, anyhow, you jest believe that punkin' coach, rats, mice, and all, when you're hearin' bout it, fore ever you stop to think it ain't so.

"I don' know how tis, but the folks in that Cinderella story seem to match together somehow; they're all pow'ful onlikely—the prince feller with the glass slipper, and the hull bunch; but jest the same you kind o' gulp em all down in a lump. But land, Rebecky, nobody'd swaller that there village maiden o' your'n, and as for what's-his-name Littlefield, that come out o' them bushes, such a feller never 'd a' be'n in bushes! No, Rebecky, you're the smartest

58

little critter there is in this township, and you beat your Uncle Jerry all holler when it comes to usin' a lead pencil, but I say that ain't no true Riverboro story! Look at the way they talk! What was that' bout being *betrothed*'?"

"Betrothed is a genteel word for engaged to be married," explained the crushed and chastened author; and it was fortunate the doting old man did not notice her eyes in the twilight, or he might have known that tears were not far away.

"Well, that's all right, then; I'm as ignorant as Cooper's cow when it comes to the dictionary. How about what's-his-name callin' the girl 'Naysweet'?"

"I thought myself that sounded foolish,:" confessed Rebecca; "but it's what the Doctor calls Cora when he tries to persuade her not to quarrel with his mother who comes to live with them. I know they don't say it in Riverboro or Temperance, but I thought perhaps it was Boston talk."

"Well, it ain't!" asserted Mr. Cobb decisively. "I've druv Boston men up in the stage from Milltown many's the time, and none of em ever said Naysweet to me, nor nothin'like it. They talked like folks, every mother's son of em! If I'd a' had that what's-his-name on the harricane deck' o' the stage and he tried any naysweetin' on me, I'd a' pitched him into the cornfield, side o' the road. I guess you ain't growed up enough for that kind of a story, Rebecky, for your poetry can't be beat in York County, that's sure, and your compositions are good enough to read out loud in town meetin' any day!"

Rebecca brightened up a little and bade the old couple her usual affectionate good night, but she descended the hill in a saddened mood. When she reached the bridge the sun, a ball of red fire, was setting behind Squire Bean's woods. As she looked, it shone full on the broad, still bosom of the river, and for one perfect instant the trees on the shores were reflected, all swimming in a sea of pink. Leaning over the rail, she watched the light fade from crimson to carmine, from carmine to rose, from rose to amber, and from amber to gray. Then withdrawing Lancelot or the Parted Lovers from her apron pocket, she tore the pages into bits and dropped them into the water below with a sigh.

59

"Uncle Jerry never said a word about the ending!" she thought; "and that was so nice!"

And she was right; but while Uncle Jerry was an illuminating critic when it came to the actions and language of his Riverboro neighbors, he had no power to direct the young mariner when she "followed the gleam," and used her imagination.

OUR SECRET SOCIETY

November, 187 —

Our Secret society has just had a splendid picnic in Candace Milliken's barn.

Our name is the B. O. S. S., and not a single boy in the village has been able to guess it. It means Braid Over Shoulder Society, and that is the sign. All the members wear one of their braids over the right shoulder in front; the president's tied with red ribbon (I am the president) and all the rest tied with blue.

To attract the attention of another member when in company or at a public place we take the braid between the thumb and little finger and stand carelessly on one leg. This is the Secret Signal and the password is Sobb (B. O. S. S. spelled backwards) which was my idea and is thought rather uncommon.

One of the rules of the B. O. S. S. is that any member may be required to tell her besetting sin at any meeting, if asked to do so by a majority of the members.

This was Candace Milliken's idea and much opposed by everybody, but when it came to a vote so many of the girls were afraid of offending Candace that they agreed because there was nobody else's father and mother who would let us picnic in their barn and use their plow, harrow, grindstone, sleigh, carryall, pung, sled, and wheelbarrow, which we did and injured hardly anything.

They asked me to tell my besetting sin at the very first meeting, and it nearly killed me to do it because it is such a common greedy one. It is that I can't bear to call the other girls when I have found a thick spot when we are out berrying in the summer time.

60

After I confessed, which made me dreadfully ashamed, every one of the girls seemed surprised and said they had never noticed that one but had each thought of something very different that I would be sure to think was my besetting sin. Then Emma Jane said that rather than tell hers she would resign from the Society and miss the picnic. So it made so much trouble that Candace gave up. We struck out the rule from the constitution and I had told my sin for nothing.

The reason we named ourselves the B. O. S. S. is that Minnie Smellie has had her head shaved after scarlet fever and has no braid, so she can't be a member.

I don't want her for a member but I can't be happy thinking she will feel slighted, and it takes away half the pleasure of belonging to the Society myself and being president.

That, I think, is the principal trouble about doing mean and unkind things; that you can't do wrong and feel right, or be bad and feel good. If you only could you could do anything that came into your mind yet always be happy.

Minnie Smellie spoils everything she comes into but I suppose we other girls must either have our hair shaved and call ourselves The Baldheadians or let her be some kind of a special officer in the B. O. S. S.

She might be the B. I. T. U. D. member (Braid in the Upper Drawer), for there is where Mrs. Smellie keeps it now that it is cut off.

WINTER THOUGHTS

March, 187—

It is not such a cold day for March and I am up in the barn chamber with my coat and hood on and Aunt Jane's waterproof and my mittens.

After I do three pages I am going to hide away this book in the haymow till spring.

Perhaps they get made into icicles on the way but I do not seem

61

to have any thoughts in the winter time. The barn chamber is full of thoughts in warm weather. The sky gives them to me, and the trees and flowers, and the birds, and the river; but now it is always gray and nipping, the branches are bare and the river is frozen.

It is too cold to write in my bedroom but while we still kept an open fire I had a few thoughts, but now there is an air-tight stove in the dining room where we sit, and we seem so close together, Aunt Miranda, Aunt Jane and I that I don't like to write in my book for fear they will ask me to read out loud my secret thoughts.

I have just read over the first part of my Thought Book and I have outgrown it all, just exactly as I have outgrown my last year's drab cashmere.

It is very queer how anybody can change so fast in a few months, but I remember that Emma Jane's cat had kittens the day my book was bought at Watson's store. Mrs. Perkins kept the prettiest white one, Abijah Flagg drowning all the others.

It seems strange to me that cats will go on having kittens when they know what becomes of them! We were very sad about it, but Mrs. Perkins said it was the way of the world and how things had to be.

I cannot help being glad that they do not do the same with children, or John and Jenny Mira Mark and me would all have had stones tied to our necks and been dropped into the deepest part of Sunny Brook, for Hannah and Fanny are the only truly handsome ones in the family.

Mrs. Perkins says I dress up well, but never being dressed up it does not matter much. At least they didn't wait to dress up the kittens to see how they would improve, before drowning them, but decided right away.

Emma Jane's kitten that was born the same day this book was is now quite an old cat who knows the way of the world herself, and how things have to be, for she has had one batch of kittens drowned already.

So perhaps it is not strange that my Thought Book seems so babyish and foolish to me when I think of all I have gone through and the millions of things I have learned, and how much better I spell than I did ten months ago.

My fingers are cold through the mittens, so good-bye dear Thought Book, friend of my childhood, now so far far behind me!

I will hide you in the haymow where you'll be warm and cosy all the long winter and where nobody can find you again in the summer time but your affectionate author,

REBECCA ROWENA RANDALL.

FOURTH CHRONICLE

A TRAGEDY IN MILLINERY

I

Emma Jane Perkins's new winter dress was a blue and green Scotch plaid poplin, trimmed with narrow green velvet-ribbon and steel nail-heads. She had a gray jacket of thick furry cloth with large steel buttons up the front, a pair of green kid gloves, and a gray felt hat with an encircling band of bright green feathers. The band began in front with a bird's head and ended behind with a bird's tail, and angels could have desired no more beautiful toilette. That was her opinion, and it was shared to the full by Rebecca.

But Emma Jane, as Rebecca had once described her to Mr. Adam Ladd, was a rich blacksmith's daughter, and she, Rebecca, was a little half-orphan from a mortgaged farm "up Temperance way," dependent upon her spinster aunts for board, clothes, and schooling. Scotch plaid poplins were manifestly not for her, but dark-colored woolen stuffs were, and mittens, and last winter's coats and furs.

And how about hats? Was there hope in store for her there? she wondered, as she walked home from the Perkins house, full of admiration for Emma Jane's winter outfit, and loyally trying to keep that admiration free from wicked envy. Her red-winged black hat was her second best, and although it was shabby she still liked it, but it would never do for church, even in Aunt Miranda's strange and never-to-be-comprehended views of suitable raiment.

There was a brown felt turban in existence, if one could call it existence when it had been rained on, snowed on, and hailed on for two seasons; but the trimmings had at any rate perished quite off the face of the earth, that was one comfort!

Emma Jane had said, rather indiscreetly, that at the village milliner's at Milliken's Mills there was a perfectly elegant pink breast to be had, a breast that began in a perfectly elegant solferino and terminated in a perfectly elegant magenta; two colors much in vogue at that time. If the old brown hat was to be her portion yet another winter, would Aunt Miranda conceal its deficiencies from a carping world beneath the shaded solferino breast? WOULD she, that was the question?

Filled with these perplexing thoughts, Rebecca entered the brick house, hung up her hood in the entry, and went into the dining-room.

Miss Jane was not there, but Aunt Miranda sat by the window with her lap full of sewing things, and a chair piled with pasteboard boxes by her side. In one hand was the ancient, battered, brown felt turban, and in the other were the orange and black porcupine quills from Rebecca's last summer's hat; from the hat of the summer before that, and the summer before that, and so on back to prehistoric ages of which her childish memory kept no specific record, though she was sure that Temperance and Riverboro society did. Truly a sight to chill the blood of any eager young dreamer who had been looking at gayer plumage!

Miss Sawyer glanced up for a second with a satisfied expression and then bent her eyes again upon her work.

"If I was going to buy a hat trimming," she said, "I couldn't select anything better or more economical than these quills! Your mother had them when she was married, and you wore them the day you come to the brick house from the farm; and I said to myself then that they looked kind of outlandish, but I've grown to like em now I've got used to em. You've been here for goin' on two years and they've hardly be'n out o'wear, summer or winter, more'n a month to a time! I declare they do beat all for service! It don't seem as if your mother could a' chose em,—Aurelia was always such a poor buyer! The black spills are bout as good as new, but the orange ones are gittin' a little mite faded and shabby. I wonder if I couldn't dip all of em in shoe blackin'? It seems real queer to put a porcupine into hat trimmin', though I declare I don't know jest what the animiles are like, it's be'n so long sence I looked at the pictures of em in a geography. I always thought their quills stood out straight and angry, but these kind o' curls round some at the

65

ends, and that makes em stand the wind better. How do you like em on the brown felt?" she asked, inclining her head in a discriminating attitude and poising them awkwardly on the hat with her work-stained hand.

How did she like them on the brown felt indeed?

Miss Sawyer had not been looking at Rebecca, but the child's eyes were flashing, her bosom heaving, and her cheeks glowing with sudden rage and despair. All at once something happened. She forgot that she was speaking to an older person; forgot that she was dependent; forgot everything but her disappointment at losing the solferino breast, remembering nothing but the enchanting, dazzling beauty of Emma Jane Perkins's winter outfit; and suddenly, quite without warning, she burst into a torrent of protest.

"I will *not* wear those hateful porcupine quills again this winter! I will not! It's wicked, *wicked* to expect me to! Oh! How I wish there never had been any porcupines in the world, or that all of them had died before silly, hateful people ever thought of trimming hat with them! They curl round and tickle my ear! They blow against my cheek and sting it like needles! They do look outlandish, you said so yourself a minute ago. Nobody ever had any but only just me! The only porcupine was made into the only quills for me and nobody else! I wish instead of sticking *out* of the nasty beasts, that they stuck *into* them, same as they do into my cheek! I suffer, suffer, suffer, wearing them and hating them, and they will last forever and forever, and when I'm dead and can't help myself, somebody'll rip them out of my last year's hat and stick them on my head, and I'll be buried in them! Well, when I am buried *they* will be, that's one good thing! Oh, if I ever have a child I'll let her choose her own feathers and not make her wear ugly things like pigs' bristles and porcupine quills!"

With this lengthy tirade Rebecca vanished like a meteor, through the door and down the street, while Miranda Sawyer gasped for breath, and prayed to Heaven to help her understand such human whirlwinds as this Randall niece of hers.

This was at three o'clock, and at half-past three Rebecca was kneeling on the rag carpet with her head in her aunt's apron, sobbing her contrition.

"Oh! Aunt Miranda, do forgive me if you can. It's the only time I've been bad for months! You know it is! You know you said last week I hadn't been any trouble lately. Something broke inside of me and came tumbling out of my mouth in ugly words! The porcupine quills make me feel just as a bull does when he sees a red cloth; nobody understands how I suffer with them!"

Miranda Sawyer had learned a few lessons in the last two years, lessons which were making her (at least on her "good days") a trifle kinder, and at any rate a juster woman than she used to be. When she alighted on the wrong side of her four-poster in the morning, or felt an extra touch of rheumatism, she was still grim and unyielding; but sometimes a curious sort of melting process seemed to go on within her, when her whole bony structure softened, and her eyes grew less vitreous. At such moments Rebecca used to feel as if a superincumbent iron pot had been lifted off her head, allowing her to breath freely and enjoy the sunshine.

"Well," she said finally, after staring first at Rebecca and then at the porcupine quills, as if to gain some insight into the situation, "well, I never, sence I was born int' the world, heerd such a speech as you've spoke, an' I guess there probably never was one. You'd better tell the minister what you said and see what he thinks of his prize Sunday-school scholar. But I'm too old and tired to scold and fuss, and try to train you same as I did at first. You can punish yourself this time, like you used to. Go fire something down the well, same as you did your pink parasol! You've apologized and we won't say no more about it today, but I expect you to show by extry good conduct how sorry you be! You care altogether too much about your looks and your clothes for a child, and you've got a temper that'll certainly land you in state's prison some o' these days!"

Rebecca wiped her eyes and laughed aloud. "No, no, Aunt Miranda, it won't, really! That wasn't temper; I don't get angry with PEOPLE; but only, once in a long while, with things; like those,— cover them up quick before I begin again! I'm all right! Shower's over, sun's out!"

Miss Miranda looked at her searchingly and

67

uncomprehendingly. Rebecca's state of mind came perilously near to disease, she thought.

"Have you seen me buyin' any new bunnits, or your Aunt Jane?" she asked cuttingly. "Is there any particular reason why you should dress better than your elders? You might as well know that we're short of cash just now, your Aunt Jane and me, and have no intention of riggin' you out like a Milltown fact'ry girl."

"Oh-h!" cried Rebecca, the quick tears starting again to her eyes and the color fading out of her cheeks, as she scrambled up from her knees to a seat on the sofa beside her aunt. "Oh-h! How ashamed I am! Quick, sew those quills on to the brown turban while I'm good! If I can't stand them I'll make a neat little gingham bag and slip over them!"

And so the matter ended, not as it customarily did, with cold words on Miss Miranda's part and bitter feelings on Rebecca's, but with a gleam of mutual understanding.

Mrs. Cobb, who was a master hand at coloring, dipped the offending quills in brown dye and left them to soak in it all night, not only making them a nice warm color, but somewhat weakening their rocky spines, so that they were not quite as rampantly hideous as before, in Rebecca's opinion.

Then Mrs. Perkins went to her bandbox in the attic and gave Miss Dearborn some pale blue velvet, with which she bound the brim of the brown turban and made a wonderful rosette, out of which the porcupine's defensive armor sprang, buoyantly and gallantly, like the plume of Henry of Navarre.

Rebecca was resigned, if not greatly comforted, but she had grace enough to conceal her feelings, now that she knew economy was at the root of some of her aunt's decrees in matters of dress; and she managed to forget the solferino breast, save in sleep, where a vision of it had a way of appearing to her, dangling from the ceiling, and dazzling her so with its rich color that she used to hope the milliner would sell it that she might never be tempted with it when she passed the shop window.

One day, not long afterward, Miss Miranda borrowed Mr. Perkins's horse and wagon and took Rebecca with her on a drive to Union, to see about some sausage meat and head cheese. She

68

intended to call on Mrs. Cobb, order a load of pine wood from Mr. Strout on the way, and leave some rags for a rug with old Mrs. Pease, so that the journey could be made as profitable as possible, consistent with the loss of time and the wear and tear on her second-best black dress.

The red-winged black hat was forcibly removed from Rebecca's head just before starting, and the nightmare turban substituted.

"You might as well begin to wear it first as last," remarked Miranda, while Jane stood in the side door and sympathized secretly with Rebecca.

"I will!" said Rebecca, ramming the stiff turban down on her head with a vindictive grimace, and snapping the elastic under her long braids; "but it makes me think of what Mr. Robinson said when the minister told him his mother-in-law would ride in the same buggy with him at his wife's funeral."

"I can't see how any speech of Mr. Robinson's, made years an' years ago, can have anything to do with wearin' your turban down to Union," said Miranda, settling the lap robe over her knees.

"Well, it can; because he said: Have it that way, then, but it'll spile the hull blamed trip for me!'"

Jane closed the door suddenly, partly because she experienced a desire to smile (a desire she had not felt for years before Rebecca came to the brick house to live), and partly because she had no wish to overhear what her sister would say when she took in the full significance of Rebecca's anecdote, which was a favorite one with Mr. Perkins.

It was a cold blustering day with a high wind that promised to bring an early fall of snow. The trees were stripped bare of leaves, the ground was hard, and the wagon wheels rattled noisily over the thank-you-ma'ams.

"I'm glad I wore my Paisley shawl over my cloak," said Miranda. "Be you warm enough, Rebecca? Tie that white rigolette tighter round your neck. The wind fairly blows through my bones. I most wish t we'd waited till a pleasanter day, for this Union road is all up hill or down, and we shan't get over the ground fast, it's so rough. Don't forget, when you go into Scott's, to say I want all the trimmin's when they send me the pork, for mebbe I can try out a

69

little mite o' lard. The last load o' pine's gone turrible quick; I must see if "Bijah Flagg can't get us some cut-rounds at the mills, when he hauls for Squire Bean next time. Keep your mind on your drivin', Rebecca, and don't look at the trees and the sky so much. It's the same sky and same trees that have been here right along. Go awful slow down this hill and walk the hoss over Cook's Brook bridge, for I always suspicion it's goin' to break down under me, an' I shouldn't want to be dropped into that fast runnin' water this cold day. It'll be froze stiff by this time next week. Hadn't you better get out and lead" —

The rest of the sentence was very possibly not vital, but at any rate it was never completed, for in the middle of the bridge a fierce gale of wind took Miss Miranda's Paisley shawl and blew it over her head. The long heavy ends whirled in opposite directions and wrapped themselves tightly about her wavering bonnet. Rebecca had the whip and the reins, and in trying to rescue her struggling aunt could not steady her own hat, which was suddenly torn from her head and tossed against the bridge rail, where it trembled and flapped for an instant.

"My hat! Oh! Aunt Miranda, my hateful hat!" cried Rebecca, never remembering at the instant how often she had prayed that the "fretful porcupine" might some time vanish in this violent manner, since it refused to die a natural death.

She had already stopped the horse, so, giving her aunt's shawl one last desperate twitch, she slipped out between the wagon wheels, and darted in the direction of the hated object, the loss of which had dignified it with a temporary value and importance.

The stiff brown turban rose in the air, then dropped and flew along the bridge; Rebecca pursued; it danced along and stuck between two of the railings; Rebecca flew after it, her long braids floating in the wind.

"Come back! Come back! Don't leave me alone with the team. I won't have it! Come back, and leave your hat!"

Miranda had at length extricated herself from the submerging shawl, but she was so blinded by the wind, and so confused that she did not measure the financial loss involved in her commands.

Rebecca heard, but her spirit being in arms, she made one more

70

mad scramble for the vagrant hat, which now seemed possessed with an evil spirit, for it flew back and forth, and bounded here and there, like a living thing, finally distinguishing itself by blowing between the horse's front and hind legs, Rebecca trying to circumvent it by going around the wagon, and meeting it on the other side.

It was no use; as she darted from behind the wheels the wind gave the hat an extra whirl, and scurrying in the opposite direction it soared above the bridge rail and disappeared into the rapid water below.

"Get in again!" cried Miranda, holding on her bonnet. "You done your best and it can't be helped, I only wish't I'd let you wear your black hat as you wanted to; and I wish't we'd never come such a day! The shawl has broke the stems of the velvet geraniums in my bonnet, and the wind has blowed away my shawl pin and my back comb. I'd like to give up and turn right back this minute, but I don't like to borrer Perkins's hoss again this month. When we get up in the woods you can smooth your hair down and tie the rigolette over your head and settle what's left of my bonnet; it'll be an expensive errant, this will!"

. . . .

II

It was not till next morning that Rebecca's heart really began its song of thanksgiving. Her Aunt Miranda announced at breakfast, that as Mrs. Perkins was going to Milliken's Mills, Rebecca might go too, and buy a serviceable hat.

"You mustn't pay over two dollars and a half, and you mustn't get the pink bird without Mrs. Perkins says, and the milliner says, that it won't fade nor moult. Don't buy a light-colored felt because you'll get sick of it in two or three years same as you did the brown

71

one. I always liked the shape of the brown one, and you'll never get another trimmin' that'll wear like them quills."

"I hope not!" thought Rebecca.

"If you had put your elastic under your chin, same as you used to, and not worn it behind because you think it's more grown-up an' fash'onable, the wind never'd a' took the hat off your head, and you wouldn't a' lost it; but the mischief's done and you can go right over to Mis' Perkins now, so you won't miss her nor keep her waitin'. The two dollars and a half is in an envelope side o' the clock."

Rebecca swallowed the last spoonful of picked-up codfish on her plate, wiped her lips, and rose from her chair happier than the seraphs in Paradise.

The porcupine quills had disappeared from her life, and without any fault or violence on her part. She was wholly innocent and virtuous, but nevertheless she was going to have a new hat with the solferino breast, should the adored object prove, under rigorous examination, to be practically indestructible.

> "Whene'er I take my walks abroad,
> How many hats I'll see;
> But if they're trimmed with hedgehog quills
> They'll not belong to me!"

So she improvised, secretly and ecstatically, as she went towards the side entry.

"There's 'Bijah Flagg drivin' in," said Miss Miranda, going to the window. "Step out and see what he's got, Jane; some passel from the Squire, I guess. It's a paper bag and it may be a punkin, though he wouldn't wrop up a punkin, come to think of it! Shet the dinin' room door, Jane; it's turrible drafty. Make haste, for the Squire's hoss never stan's still a minute cept when he's goin'!"

Abijah Flagg alighted and approached the side door with a grin.

"Guess what I've got for ye, Rebecky?"

No throb of prophetic soul warned Rebecca of her approaching doom.

"Nodhead apples?" she sparkled, looking as bright and rosy and satin-skinned as an apple herself.

"No; guess again."

"A flowering geranium?"

"Guess again!"

"Nuts? Oh! I can't, Bijah; I'm just going to Milliken's Mills on an errand, and I'm afraid of missing Mrs. Perkins. Show me quick! Is it really for me, or for Aunt Miranda?"

"Reely for you, I guess!" and he opened the large brown paper bag and drew from it the remains of a water-soaked hat!

They WERE remains, but there was no doubt of their nature and substance. They had clearly been a hat in the past, and one could even suppose that, when resuscitated, they might again assume their original form in some near and happy future.

Miss Miranda, full of curiosity, joined the group in the side entry at this dramatic moment.

"Well, I never!" she exclaimed. "Where, and how under the canopy, did you ever?"

"I was working on the dam at Union Falls yesterday," chuckled Abijah, with a pleased glance at each of the trio in turn, "an' I seen this little bunnit skippin' over the water jest as Becky does over the road. It's shaped kind o' like a boat, an' gorry, ef it wa'nt sailin' jest like a boat! Where hev I seen that kind of a bristlin' plume?' thinks I."

("Where indeed!" thought Rebecca stormily.)

"Then it come to me that I'd drove that plume to school and drove it to meetin' and drove it to the Fair an'drove it most everywheres on Becky. So I reached out a pole an' ketched it fore it got in amongst the logs an' come to any damage, an' here it is! The hat's passed in its checks, I guess; looks kind as if a wet elephant had stepped on it; but the plume's bout's good as new! I reely fetched the hat beck for the sake o' the plume."

"It was real good of you, 'Bijah, an' we're all of us obliged to you," said Miranda, as she poised the hat on one hand and turned it slowly with the other.

"Well, I do say," she exclaimed, "and I guess I've said it before, that of all the wearing' plumes that ever I see, that one's the

73

wearin'est! Seems though it just wouldn't give up. Look at the way it's held Mis' Cobb's dye; it's about as brown's when it went int' the water."

"Dyed, but not a mite dead," grinned Abijah, who was somewhat celebrated for his puns.

"And I declare," Miranda continued, "when you think o' the fuss they make about ostriches, killin' em off by hundreds for the sake o' their feathers that'll string out and spoil in one hard rainstorm,—an' all the time lettin' useful porcupines run round with their quills on, why I can't hardly understand it, without milliners have found out jest how good they do last, an' so they won't use em for trimmin'. 'Bijah's right; the hat ain't no more use, Rebecca, but you can buy you another this mornin'—any color or shape you fancy—an' have Miss Morton sew these brown quills on to it with some kind of a buckle or a bow, jest to hide the roots. Then you'll be fixed for another season, thanks to 'Bijah."

Uncle Jerry and Aunt Sarah Cobb were made acquainted before very long with the part that destiny, or Abijah Flagg, had played in Rebecca's affairs, for, accompanied by the teacher, she walked to the old stage driver's that same afternoon. Taking off her new hat with the venerable trimming, she laid it somewhat ostentatiously upside down on the kitchen table and left the room, dimpling a little more than usual.

Uncle Jerry rose from his seat, and, crossing the room, looked curiously into the hat and found that a circular paper lining was neatly pinned in the crown, and that it bore these lines, which were read aloud with great effect by Miss Dearborn, and with her approval were copied in the Thought Book for the benefit of posterity:

> *"It was the bristling porcupine,*
> *As he stood on his native heath,*
> *He said, 'I'll pluck me some immortelles*
> *And make me up a wreath.*
> *For tho' I may not live myself*
> *To more than a hundred and ten,*
> *My quills will last till crack of doom,*

74

And maybe after then.
They can be colored blue or green
Or orange, brown, or red,
But often as they may be dyed
They never will be dead.'
And so the bristling porcupine
As he stood on his native heath,
Said, I think I'll pluck me some immmortelles
And make me up a wreath.'

"R. R. R."

FIFTH CHRONICLE

THE SAVING OF THE COLORS

I

Even when Rebecca had left school, having attained the great age of seventeen and therefore able to look back over a past incredibly long and full, she still reckoned time not by years, but by certain important occurrences.

There was the year her father died; the year she left Sunnybrook Farm to come to her aunts in Riverboro; the year Sister Hannah became engaged; the year little Mira died; the year Abijah Flagg ceased to be Squire Bean's chore-boy, and astounded Riverboro by departing for Limerick Academy in search of an education; and finally the year of her graduation, which, to the mind of seventeen, seems rather the culmination than the beginning of existence.

Between these epoch-making events certain other happenings stood out in bold relief against the gray of dull daily life.

There was the day she first met her friend of friends, "Mr. Aladdin," and the later, even more radiant one when he gave her the coral necklace. There was the day the Simpson family moved away from Riverboro under a cloud, and she kissed Clara Belle fervently at the cross-roads, telling her that she would always be faithful. There was the visit of the Syrian missionaries to the brick house. That was a bright, romantic memory, as strange and brilliant as the wonderful little birds' wings and breasts that the strangers brought from the Far East. She remembered the moment they asked her to choose some for herself, and the rapture with which she stroked the beautiful things as they lay on the black haircloth sofa. Then there was the coming of the new minister, for though many were tried only one was chosen; and finally there was the flag-raising, a festivity that thrilled Riverboro and Edgewood society

76

from centre to circumference, a festivity that took place just before she entered the Female Seminary at Wareham and said good-by to kind Miss Dearborn and the village school.

There must have been other flag-raisings in history,—even the persons most interested in this particular one would grudgingly have allowed that much,—but it would have seemed to them improbable that any such flag-raising as theirs, either in magnitude of conception or brilliancy of actual performance, could twice glorify the same century. Of some pageants it is tacitly admitted that there can be no duplicates, and the flag-raising at Riverboro Centre was one of these; so that it is small wonder if Rebecca chose it as one of the important dates in her personal almanac.

The new minister's wife was the being, under Providence, who had conceived the germinal idea of the flag.

At this time the parish had almost settled down to the trembling belief that they were united on a pastor. In the earlier time a minister was chosen for life, and if he had faults, which was a probably enough contingency, and if his congregation had any, which is within the bounds of possibility, each bore with the other (not quite without friction), as old-fashioned husbands and wives once did, before the easy way out of the difficulty was discovered, or at least before it was popularized.

The faithful old parson had died after thirty years' preaching, and perhaps the newer methods had begun to creep in, for it seemed impossible to suit the two communities most interested in the choice.

The Rev. Mr. Davis, for example, was a spirited preacher, but persisted in keeping two horses in the parsonage stable, and in exchanging them whenever he could get faster ones. As a parochial visitor he was incomparable, dashing from house to house with such speed that he could cover the parish in a single afternoon. This sporting tendency, which would never have been remarked in a British parson, was frowned upon in a New England village, and Deacon Milliken told Mr. Davis, when giving him what he alluded to as his "walking papers," that they didn't want the Edgewood church run by hoss power!

The next candidate pleased Edgewood, where morning

preaching was held, but the other parish, which had afternoon service, declined to accept him because he wore a wig—an ill-matched, crookedly applied wig.

Number three was eloquent but given to gesticulation, and Mrs. Jere Burbank, the president of the Dorcas Society, who sat in a front pew, said she couldn't bear to see a preacher scramble round the pulpit hot Sundays.

Number four, a genial, handsome man, gifted in prayer, was found to be a Democrat. The congregation was overwhelmingly Republican in its politics, and perceived something ludicrous, if not positively blasphemous, in a Democrat preaching the gospel. ("Ananias and Beelzebub'll be candidatin' here, first thing we know!" exclaimed the outraged Republican nominee for district attorney.)

Number five had a feeble-minded child, which the hiring committee prophesied, would always be standing in the parsonage front yard, making talk for the other denominations.

Number six was the Rev. Judson Baxter, the present incumbent; and he was voted to be as near perfection as a minister can be in this finite world. His young wife had a small income of her own, a distinct and unusual advantage, and the subscription committee hoped that they might not be eternally driving over the country to get somebody's fifty cents that had been over-due for eight months, but might take their onerous duties a little more easily.

"It does seem as if our ministers were the poorest lot!" complained Mrs. Robinson. "If their salary is two months behindhand they begin to be nervous! Seems as though they might lay up a little before they come here, and not live from hand to mouth so! The Baxters seem quite different, and I only hope they won't get wasteful and run into debt. They say she keeps the parlor blinds open bout half the time, and the room is lit up so often evenin's that the neighbors think her and Mr. Baxter must set in there. It don't seem hardly as if it could be so, but Mrs. Buzzell says tis, and she says we might as well say good-by to the parlor carpet, which is church property, for the Baxters are living all over it!"

This criticism was the only discordant note in the chorus of

78

praise, and the people gradually grew accustomed to the open blinds and the overused parlor carpet, which was just completing its twenty-fifth year of honest service.

Mrs. Baxter communicated her patriotic idea of a new flag to the Dorcas Society, proposing that the women should cut and make it themselves.

"It may not be quite as good as those manufactured in the large cities," she said, "but we shall be proud to see our home-made flag flying in the breeze, and it will mean all the more to the young voters growing up, to remember that their mothers made it with their own hands."

"How would it do to let some of the girls help?" modestly asked Miss Dearborn, the Riverboro teacher. "We might choose the best sewers and let them put in at least a few stitches, so that they can feel they have a share in it."

"Just the thing!" exclaimed Mrs. Baxter. "We can cut the stripes and sew them together, and after we have basted on the white stars the girls can apply them to the blue ground. We must have it ready for the campaign rally, and we couldn't christen it at a better time than in this presidential year."

II

In this way the great enterprise was started, and day by day the preparations went forward in the two villages.

The boys, as future voters and fighters, demanded an active share in the proceedings, and were organized by Squire Bean into a fife and drum corps, so that by day and night martial but most inharmonious music woke the echoes, and deafened mothers felt their patriotism oozing out at the soles of their shoes.

Dick Carter was made captain, for his grandfather had a gold medal given him by Queen Victoria for rescuing three hundred and twenty-six passengers from a sinking British vessel. Riverboro thought it high time to pay some graceful tribute to Great Britain in return for her handsome conduct to Captain Nahum Carter, and human imagination could contrive nothing more impressive than a vicarious share in the flag raising.

Living Perkins tried to be happy in the ranks, for he was offered no official position, principally, Mrs. Smellie observed, because "his father's war record wa'nt clean." "Oh, yes! Jim Perkins went to the war," she continued. "He hid out behind the hencoop when they was draftin', but they found him and took him along. He got into one battle, too, somehow or nother, but he run away from it. He was allers cautious, Jim was; if he ever see trouble of any kind comin' towards him, he was out o' sight fore it got a chance to light. He said eight dollars a month, without bounty, wouldn't pay HIM to stop bullets for. He wouldn't fight a skeeter, Jim wouldn't, but land! we ain't to war all the time, and he's a good neighbor and a good blacksmith."

Miss Dearborn was to be Columbia and the older girls of the two schools were to be the States. Such trade in muslins and red, white, and blue ribbons had never been known since "Watson kep' store," and the number of brief white petticoats hanging out to bleach would have caused the passing stranger to imagine Riverboro a continual dancing school.

Juvenile virtue, both male and female, reached an almost impossible height, for parents had only to lift a finger and say, "you shan't go to the flag raising!" and the refractory spirit at once armed itself for new struggles toward the perfect life.

Mr. Jeremiah Cobb had consented to impersonate Uncle Sam, and was to drive Columbia and the States to the "raising" on the top of his own stage. Meantime the boys were drilling, the ladies were cutting and basting and stitching, and the girls were sewing on stars; for the starry part of the spangled banner was to remain with each of them in turn until she had performed her share of the work.

It was felt by one and all a fine and splendid service indeed to help in the making of the flag, and if Rebecca was proud to be of the chosen ones, so was her Aunt Jane Sawyer, who had taught her all her delicate stitches.

On a long-looked-for afternoon in August the minister's wife

80

drove up to the brick house door, and handed out the great piece of bunting to Rebecca, who received it in her arms with as much solemnity as if it had been a child awaiting baptismal rites.

"I'm so glad!" she sighed happily. "I thought it would never come my turn!"

"You should have had it a week ago, but Huldah Meserve upset the ink bottle over her star, and we had to baste on another one. You are the last, though, and then we shall sew the stars and stripes together, and Seth Strout will get the top ready for hanging. Just think, it won't be many days before you children will be pulling the rope with all your strength, the band will be playing, the men will be cheering, and the new flag will go higher and higher, till the red, white, and blue shows against the sky!"

Rebecca's eyes fairly blazed. "Shall I fell on' my star, or buttonhole it?" she asked.

"Look at all the others and make the most beautiful stitches you can, that's all. It is your star, you know, and you can even imagine it is your state, and try and have it the best of all. If everybody else is trying to do the same thing with her state, that will make a great country, won't it?"

Rebecca's eyes spoke glad confirmation of the idea. "My star, my state!" she repeated joyously. "Oh, Mrs. Baxter, I'll make such fine stitches you'll think the white grew out of the blue!"

The new minister's wife looked pleased to see her spark kindle a flame in the young heart. "You can sew so much of yourself into your star," she went on in the glad voice that made her so winsome, "that when you are an old lady you can put on your specs and find it among all the others. Good-by! Come up to the parsonage Saturday afternoon; Mr. Baxter wants to see you."

"Judson, help that dear little genius of a Rebecca all you can!" she said that night, when they were cosily talking in their parlor and living "all over" the parish carpet. "I don't know what she may, or may not, come to, some day; I only wish she were ours! If you could have seen her clasp the flag tight in her arms and put her cheek against it, and watched the tears of feeling start in her eyes when I told her that her star was her state! I kept whispering to myself, Covet not thy neighbor's child!'"

81

Daily at four o'clock Rebecca scrubbed her hands almost to the bone, brushed her hair, and otherwise prepared herself in body, mind, and spirit for the consecrated labor of sewing on her star. All the time that her needle cautiously, conscientiously formed the tiny stitches she was making rhymes "in her head," her favorite achievement being this:—

"Your star, my star, all our stars together,
They make the dear old banner proud
To float in the bright fall weather."

There was much discussion as to which of the girls should impersonate the State of Maine, for that was felt to be the highest honor in the gift of the committee.

Alice Robinson was the prettiest child in the village, but she was very shy and by no means a general favorite.

Minnie Smellie possessed the handsomest dress and a pair of white slippers and open-work stockings that nearly carried the day. Still, as Miss Delia Weeks well said, she was so stupid that if she should suck her thumb in the very middle of the exercises nobody'd be a dite surprised!

Huldah Meserve was next voted upon, and the fact that if she were not chosen her father might withdraw his subscription to the brass band fund was a matter for grave consideration.

"I kind o' hate to have such a giggler for the State of Maine; let her be the Goddess of Liberty," proposed Mrs. Burbank, whose patriotism was more local than national.

"How would Rebecca Randall do for Maine, and let her speak some of her verses?" suggested the new minister's wife, who, could she have had her way, would have given all the prominent parts to Rebecca, from Uncle Sam down.

So, beauty, fashion, and wealth having been tried and found wanting, the committee discussed the claims of talent, and it transpired that to the awe-stricken Rebecca fell the chief plum in the pudding. It was a tribute to her gifts that there was no jealousy or envy among the other girls; they readily conceded her special fitness for the role.

Her life had not been pressed down full to the brim of pleasures, and she had a sort of distrust of joy in the bud. Not until she saw it in full radiance of bloom did she dare embrace it. She had never read any verse but Byron, Felicia Hemans, bits of "Paradise Lost," and the selections in the school readers, but she would have agreed heartily with the poet who said:—

"Not by appointment do we meet delight
And joy; they heed not our expectancy;
But round some corner in the streets of life
They on a sudden clasp us with a smile."

For many nights before the raising, when she went to her bed she said to herself, after she had finished her prayers: "It can't be true that I'm chosen for the State of Maine! It just *can't* be true! Nobody could be good *enough*, but oh, I'll try to be as good as I can! To be going to Wareham Seminary next week and to be the State of Maine too! Oh! I must pray *hard* to God to keep me meek and humble!"

III

The flag was to be raised on a Tuesday, and on the previous Sunday it became known to the children that Clara Belle Simpson was coming back from Acreville, coming to live with Mrs. Fogg and take care of the baby, called by the neighborhood boys "the Fogg horn," on account of his excellent voice production.

Clara Belle was one of Miss Dearborn's original flock, and if she were left wholly out of the festivities she would be the only girl of suitable age to be thus slighted; it seemed clear to the juvenile mind, therefore, that neither she nor her descendants would ever recover from such a blow. But, under all the circumstances, would she be allowed to join in the procession? Even Rebecca, the optimistic, feared not, and the committee confirmed her fears by saying that Abner Simpson's daughter certainly could not take any

83

prominent part in the ceremony, but they hoped that Mrs. Fogg would allow her to witness it.

When Abner Simpson, urged by the town authorities, took his wife and seven children away from Riverboro to Acreville, just over the border in the next county, Riverboro went to bed leaving its barn and shed doors unfastened, and drew long breaths of gratitude to Providence.

Of most winning disposition and genial manners, Mr. Simpson had not that instinctive comprehension of property rights which renders a man a valuable citizen.

Squire Bean was his nearest neighbor, and he conceived the novel idea of paying Simpson five dollars a year not to steal from him, a method occasionally used in the Highlands in the early days.

The bargain was struck, and adhered to religiously for a twelve-month, but on the second of January Mr. Simpson announced the verbal contract as formally broken.

"I didn't know what I was doin' when I made it, Squire," he urged. "In the first place, it's a slur on my reputation and an injury to my self-respect. Secondly, it's a nervous strain on me; and thirdly, five dollars don't pay me!"

Squire Bean was so struck with the unique and convincing nature of these arguments that he could scarcely restrain his admiration, and he confessed to himself afterward, that unless Simpson's mental attitude could be changed he was perhaps a fitter subject for medical science than the state prison.

Abner was a most unusual thief, and conducted his operations with a tact and neighborly consideration none too common in the profession. He would never steal a man's scythe in haying-time, nor his fur lap-robe in the coldest of the winter. The picking of a lock offered no attractions to him; "he wa'n't no burglar," he would have scornfully asserted. A strange horse and wagon hitched by the roadside was the most flagrant of his thefts; but it was the small things—the hatchet or axe on the chopping-block, the tin pans sunning at the side door, a stray garment bleaching on the grass, a hoe, rake, shovel, or a bag of early potatoes, that tempted him most sorely; and these appealed to him not so much for their intrinsic value as because they were so excellently adapted to swapping. The swapping was really the enjoyable part of the procedure, the theft was only a sad but necessary preliminary; for if Abner himself had been a man of sufficient property to carry on his business operations independently, it is doubtful if he would have helped himself so freely to his neighbor's goods.

Riverboro regretted the loss of Mrs. Simpson, who was useful in scrubbing, cleaning, and washing, and was thought to exercise some influence over her predatory spouse. There was a story of their early married life, when they had a farm; a story to the effect that Mrs. Simpson always rode on every load of hay that her husband took to Milltown, with the view of keeping him sober through the day. After he turned out of the country road and approached the metropolis, it was said that he used to bury the docile lady in the load. He would then drive on to the scales, have the weight of the hay entered in the buyer's book, take his horses to the stable for feed and water, and when a favorable opportunity offered he would assist the hot and panting Mrs. Simpson out of the side or back of the rack, and gallantly brush the straw from her person. For this reason it was always asserted that Abner Simpson sold his wife every time he went to Milltown, but the story was never fully substantiated, and at all events it was the only suspected blot on meek Mrs. Simpson's personal reputation.

As for the Simpson children, they were missed chiefly as familiar figures by the roadside; but Rebecca honestly loved Clara Belle, notwithstanding her Aunt Miranda's opposition to the intimacy. Rebecca's "taste for low company" was a source of continual anxiety to her aunt.

"Anything that's human flesh is good enough for her!" Miranda groaned to Jane. "She'll ride with the rag-sack-and-bottle peddler just as quick as she would with the minister; she always sets beside the St. Vitus' dance young one at Sabbath school; and she's forever riggin' and onriggin' that dirty Simpson baby! She reminds me of a puppy that'll always go to everybody that'll have him!"

It was thought very creditable to Mrs. Fogg that she sent for Clara Belle to live with her and go to school part of the year.

"She'll be useful" said Mrs. Fogg, "and she'll be out of her father's way, and so keep honest; though she's no awful hombly I've no fears for her. A girl with her red hair, freckles, and cross-eyes can't fall into no kind of sin, I don't believe."

Mrs. Fogg requested that Clara Belle should be started on her journey from Acreville by train and come the rest of the way by stage, and she was disturbed to receive word on Sunday that Mr. Simpson had borrowed a "good roader" from a new acquaintance, and would himself drive the girl from Acreville to Riverboro, a distance of thirty-five miles. That he would arrive in their vicinity on the very night before the flag-raising was thought by Riverboro to be a public misfortune, and several residents hastily determined to deny themselves a sight of the festivities and remain watchfully on their own premises.

On Monday afternoon the children were rehearsing their songs at the meeting-house. As Rebecca came out on the broad wooden steps she watched Mrs. Peter Meserve's buggy out of sight, for in front, wrapped in a cotton sheet, lay the previous flag. After a few chattering good-bys and weather prophecies with the other girls, she started on her homeward walk, dropping in at the parsonage to read her verses to the minister.

He welcomed her gladly as she removed her white cotton gloves (hastily slipped on outside the door, for ceremony) and pushed back the funny hat with the yellow and black porcupine quills—the hat with which she made her first appearance in Riverboro society.

"You've heard the beginning, Mr. Baxter; now will you please tell me if you like the last verse?" she asked, taking out her paper. "I've only read it to Alice Robinson, and I think perhaps she can never be a poet, though she's a splendid writer. Last year when she was twelve she wrote a birthday poem to herself, and she made natal' rhyme with Milton,.' which, of course, it wouldn't. I remember every verse ended:

> 'This is my day so natal
> And I will follow Milton.'

Another one of hers was written just because she couldn't help it, she said. This was it:

> 'Let me to the hills away,
> Give me pen and paper;
> I'll write until the earth will sway
> The story of my Maker.'"

The minister could scarcely refrain from smiling, but he controlled himself that he might lose none of Rebecca's quaint observations. When she was perfectly at ease, unwatched and uncriticised, she was a marvelous companion.

"The name of the poem is going to be My Star,'" she continued, "and Mrs. Baxter gave me all the ideas, but somehow there's a kind of magicness when they get into poetry, don't you think so?" (Rebecca always talked to grown people as if she were their age, or, a more subtle and truer distinction, as if they were hers.)

"It has often been so remarked, in different words," agreed the minister.

"Mrs. Baxter said that each star was a state, and if each state did its
best we should have a splendid country. Then once she said that we ought to be glad the war is over and the States are all at peace together; and I thought Columbia must be glad, too, for Miss Dearborn says she's the mother of all the States. So I'm going to have it end like this: I didn't write it, I just sewed it while I was working on my star:

> For it's your star, my star, all the stars together,
> That make our country's flag so proud
> To float in the bright fall weather.
> Northern stars, Southern stars, stars of the East and West,
> Side by side they lie at peace
> On the dear flag's mother-breast."

"'Oh! many are the poets that are sown by nature,'" thought the minister, quoting Wordsworth to himself. "And I wonder what

87

becomes of them! That's a pretty idea, little Rebecca, and I don't know whether you or my wife ought to have the more praise. What made you think of the stars lying on the flag's mother-breast'? Where did you get that word?"

"Why" (and the young poet looked rather puzzled), "that's the way it is; the flag is the whole country—the mother—and the stars are the states. The stars had to lie somewhere: '*lap*' nor '*arms*' wouldn't sound well with West,' so, of course, I said '*breast*,'" Rebecca answered, with some surprise at the question; and the minister put his hand under her chin and kissed her softly on the forehead when he said good-by at the door.

IV

Rebecca walked rapidly along in the gathering twilight, thinking of the eventful morrow.

As she approached the turning on the left called the old Milltown road, she saw a white horse and wagon, driven by a man with a rakish, flapping, Panama hat, come rapidly around the turn and disappear over the long hills leading down to the falls. There was no mistaking him; there never was another Abner Simpson, with his lean height, his bushy reddish hair, the gay cock of his hat, and the long piratical, upturned mustaches, which the boys used to say were used as hat-racks by the Simpson children at night.. The old Milltown road ran past Mrs. Fogg's house, so he must have left Clara Belle there, and Rebecca's heart glowed to think that her poor little friend need not miss the raising.

She began to run now, fearful of being late for supper, and covered the ground to the falls in a brief time. As she crossed the bridge she again saw Abner Simpson's team, drawn up at the watering trough.

Coming a little nearer, with the view of inquiring for the family, her quick eye caught sight of something unexpected. A gust of wind blew up a corner of a linen lap-robe in the back of the wagon, and underneath it she distinctly saw the white-sheeted bundle that held the flag; the bundle with a tiny, tiny spot of red bunting peeping out at one corner. It is true she had eaten, slept, dreamed red, white, and blue for weeks, but there was no mistaking the evidence of her senses; the idolized flag, longed for, worked for, sewed for, that flag was in the back of Abner Simpson's wagon, and if so, what would become of the raising?

Acting on blind impulse, she ran toward the watering-trough, calling out in her clear treble: "Mr. Simpson! Oh, Mr. Simpson, will you let me ride a piece with you and hear all about Clara Belle? I'm going part way over to the Centre on an errand." (So she was; a most important errand,—to recover the flag of her country at present in the hands of the foe!)

Mr. Simpson turned round in his seat and cried heartily, "Certain sure I will!" for he liked the fair sex, young and old, and Rebecca had always been a prime favorite with him. "Climb right in! How's everybody? Glad to see ye! The folks talk bout ye from sun-up to sun-down, and Clara Belle can't hardly wait for a sight of ye!"

Rebecca scrambled up, trembling and pale with excitement. She did not in the least know what was going to happen, but she was sure that the flag, when in the enemy's country, must be at least a little safer with the State of Maine sitting on top of it!

Mr. Simpson began a long monologue about Acreville, the house he lived in, the pond in front of it, Mrs. Simpson's health, and various items of news about the children, varied by reports of his personal misfortunes. He put no questions, and asked no replies, so this gave the inexperienced soldier a few seconds to plan a campaign. There were three houses to pass; the Browns' at the corner, the Millikens', and the Robinsons' on the brow of the hill. If Mr. Robinson were in the front yard she might tell Mr. Simpson she wanted to call there and ask Mr. Robinson to hold the horse's head while she got out of the wagon. Then she might fly to the back before Mr. Simpson could realize the situation, and dragging out the precious bundle, sit on it hard, while Mr. Robinson settled the matter of ownership with Mr. Simpson.

This was feasible, but it meant a quarrel between the two men,

89

who held an ancient grudge against each other, and Mr. Simpson was a valiant fighter as the various sheriffs who had attempted to arrest him could cordially testify. It also meant that everybody in the village would hear of the incident and poor Clara Belle be branded again as the child of a thief.

Another idea danced into her excited brain; such a clever one she could hardly believe it hers. She might call Mr. Robinson to the wagon, and when he came close to the wheels she might say, "all of a sudden": "Please take the flag out of the back of the wagon, Mr. Robinson. We have brought it here for you to keep overnight." Mr. Simpson might be so surprised that he would give up his prize rather than be suspected of stealing.

But as they neared the Robinsons' house there was not a sign of life to be seen; so the last plan, ingenious though it was, was perforce abandoned.

The road now lay between thick pine woods with no dwelling in sight. It was growing dusk and Rebecca was driving along the lonely way with a person who was generally called Slippery Simpson.

Not a thought of fear crossed her mind, save the fear of bungling in her diplomacy, and so losing the flag. She knew Mr. Simpson well, and a pleasanter man was seldom to be met. She recalled an afternoon when he came home and surprised the whole school playing the Revolutionary War in his helter-skelter dooryard, and the way in which he had joined the British forces and impersonated General Burgoyne had greatly endeared him to her. The only difficulty was to find proper words for her delicate mission, for, of course, if Mr. Simpson's anger were aroused, he would politely push her out of the wagon and drive away with the flag. Perhaps if she led the conversation in the right direction an opportunity would present itself. She well remembered how Emma Jane Perkins had failed to convert Jacob Moody, simply because she failed to "lead up" to the delicate question of his manner of life. Clearing her throat nervously, she began: "Is it likely to be fair tomorrow?"

"Guess so; clear as a bell. What's on foot; a picnic?"

"No; we're to have a grand flag-raising!" ("That is," she thought, "if we have any flag to raise!")

"That so? Where?"

"The three villages are to club together and have a rally, and raise the flag at the Centre. There'll be a brass band, and speakers, and the Mayor of Portland, and the man that will be governor if he's elected, and a dinner in the Grange Hall, and we girls are chosen to raise the flag."

"I want to know! That'll be grand, won't it?" (Still not a sign of consciousness on the part of Abner.)

"I hope Mrs. Fogg will take Clara Belle, for it will be splendid to look at! Mr. Cobb is going to be Uncle Sam and drive us on the stage. Miss Dearborn—Clara Belle's old teacher, you know—is going to be Columbia; the girls will be the States of the Union, and oh, Mr. Simpson, I am the one to be the State of Maine!" (This was not altogether to the point, but a piece of information impossible to conceal.)

Mr. Simpson flourished the whipstock and gave a loud, hearty laugh. Then he turned in his seat and regarded Rebecca curiously. "You're kind of small, hain't ye, for so big a state as this one?" he asked.

"Any of us would be too small," replied Rebecca with dignity, "but the committee asked me, and I am going to try hard to do well."

The tragic thought that there might be no occasion for anybody to do anything, well or ill, suddenly overcame her here, and putting her hand on Mr. Simpson's sleeve, she attacked the subject practically and courageously.

"Oh, Mr. Simpson, dear Mr. Simpson, it's such a mortifying subject I can't bear to say anything about it, but please give us back our flag! Don't, *don't* take it over to Acreville, Mr. Simpson! We've worked so long to make it, and it was so hard getting the money for the bunting! Wait a minute, please; don't be angry, and don't say no just yet, till I explain more. It'll be so dreadful for everybody to get there tomorrow morning and find no flag to raise, and the band and the mayor all disappointed, and the children crying, with their

91

muslin dresses all bought for nothing! O dear Mr. Simpson, please don't take our flag away from us!"

The apparently astonished Abner pulled his mustaches and exclaimed: "But I don't know what you're drivin' at! Who's got yer flag? I hain't!"

Could duplicity, deceit, and infamy go any further, Rebecca wondered, and her soul filling with righteous wrath, she cast discretion to the winds and spoke a little more plainly, bending her great swimming eyes on the now embarrassed Abner, who looked like an angle-worm, wriggling on a pin.

"Mr. Simpson, how can you say that, when I saw the flag in the back of your wagon myself, when you stopped to water the horse? It's wicked of you to take it, and I cannot bear it!" (Her voice broke now, for a doubt of Mr. Simpson's yielding suddenly darkened her mind.) "If you keep it, you'll have to keep me, for I won't be parted from it! I can't fight like the boys, but I can pinch and scratch, and I WILL scratch, just like a panther—I'll lie right down on my star and not move, if I starve to death!"

"Look here, hold your hosses n' don't cry till you git something to cry for!" grumbled the outraged Abner, to whom a clue had just come; and leaning over the wagon-back he caught hold of a corner of white sheet and dragged up the bundle, scooping off Rebecca's hat in the process, and almost burying her in bunting.

She caught the treasure passionately to her heart and stifled her sobs in it, while Abner exclaimed: "I swan to man, if that hain't a flag! Well, in that case you're good n' welcome to it! Land! I seen that bundle lyin' in the middle o' the road and I says to myself, that's somebody's washin' and I'd better pick it up and leave it at the post-office to be claimed; n' all the time it was a flag!"

This was a Simpsonian version of the matter, the fact being that a white-covered bundle lying on the Meserves' front steps had attracted his practiced eye, and slipping in at the open gate he had swiftly and deftly removed it to his wagon on general principles; thinking if it were clean clothes it would be extremely useful, and in any event there was no good in passing by something flung into your very arms, so to speak. He had had no leisure to examine the bundle, and indeed took little interest in it. Probably he stole it

92

simply from force of habit, and because there was nothing else in sight to steal, everybody's premises being preternaturally tidy and empty, almost as if his visit had been expected!

Rebecca was a practical child, and it seemed to her almost impossible that so heavy a bundle should fall out of Mrs. Meserve's buggy and not be noticed; but she hoped that Mr. Simpson was telling the truth, and she was too glad and grateful to doubt anyone at the moment.

"Thank you, thank you ever so much, Mr. Simpson. You're the nicest, kindest, politest man I ever knew, and the girls will be so pleased you gave us back the flag, and so will the Dorcas Society; they'll be sure to write you a letter of thanks; they always do."

"Tell em not to bother bout any thanks," said Simpson, beaming virtuously. "But land! I'm glad twas me that happened to see that bundle in the road and take the trouble to pick it up." ("Jest to think of it's bein' a flag!" he thought; "if ever there was a pesky, wuthless thing to trade off, twould be a great, gormin' flag like that!")

"Can I get out now, please?" asked Rebecca. "I want to go back, for Mrs. Meserve will be dreadfully nervous when she finds out she dropped the flag, and she has heart trouble."

"No, you don't," objected Mr. Simpson gallantly, turning the horse. "Do you think I'd let a little creeter like you lug that great heavy bundle? I hain't got time to go back to Meserve's, but I'll take you to the corner and dump you there, flag n' all, and you can get some o' the men-folks to carry it the rest o' the way. You'll wear it out, huggin' it so!"

"I helped make it and I adore it!" said Rebecca, who was in a high-pitched and grandiloquent mood. "Why don't YOU like it? It's your country's flag."

Simpson smiled an indulgent smile and looked a trifle bored at these frequent appeals to his extremely rusty higher feelings.

"I don' know's I've got any partic'lar int'rest in the country," he remarked languidly. "I know I don't owe nothin' to it, nor own nothin' in it!"

"You own a star on the flag, same as everybody," argued

93

Rebecca, who had been feeding on patriotism for a month; "and you own a state, too, like all of us!"

"Land! I wish't I did! or even a quarter section!" sighed Mr. Simpson, feeling somehow a little more poverty-stricken and discouraged than usual.

As they approached the corner and the watering-trough where four cross-roads met, the whole neighborhood seemed to be in evidence, and Mr. Simpson suddenly regretted his chivalrous escort of Rebecca; especially when, as he neared the group, an excited lady, wringing her hands, turned out to be Mrs. Peter Meserve, accompanied by Huldah, the Browns, Mrs. Milliken, Abijah Flagg, and Miss Dearborn.

"Do you know anything about the new flag, Rebecca?" shrieked Mrs. Meserve, too agitated, at the moment, to notice the child's companion.

"It's right here in my lap, all safe," responded Rebecca joyously.

"You careless, meddlesome young one, to take it off my steps where I left it just long enough to go round to the back and hunt up my door-key! You've given me a fit of sickness with my weak heart, and what business was it of yours? I believe you think you OWN the flag! Hand it over to me this minute!"

Rebecca was climbing down during this torrent of language, but as she turned she flashed one look of knowledge at the false Simpson, a look that went through him from head to foot, as if it were carried by electricity.

He had not deceived her after all, owing to the angry chatter of Mrs. Meserve. He had been handcuffed twice in his life, but no sheriff had ever discomfited him so thoroughly as this child. Fury mounted to his brain, and as soon as she was safely out from between the wheels he stood up in the wagon and flung the flag out in the road in the midst of the excited group.

"Take it, you pious, passimonious, cheese-parin', hair-splittin', back-bitin', flag-raisin' crew!" he roared. "Rebecca never took the flag; I found it in the road, I say!"

"You never, no such a thing!" exclaimed Mrs. Meserve. "You found it on the doorsteps in my garden!"

94

"Mebbe twas your garden, but it was so chock full o' weeks I *thought* t was the road," retorted Abner. "I vow I wouldn't a' given the old rag back to one o' *you*, not if you begged me on your bended knees! But Rebecca's a friend o' my folks and can do with her flag's she's a mind to, and the rest o' ye can go to thunder—n' stay there, for all I care!"

So saying, he made a sharp turn, gave the gaunt white horse a lash and disappeared in a cloud of dust, before the astonished Mr. Brown, the only man in the party, had a thought of detaining him.

"I'm sorry I spoke so quick, Rebecca," said Mrs. Meserve, greatly mortified at the situation. "But don't you believe a word that lyin' critter said! He did steal it off my doorstep, and how did you come to be ridin' and consortin' with him! I believe it would kill your Aunt Miranda if she should hear about it!"

The little school-teacher put a sheltering arm round Rebecca as Mr. Brown picked up the flag and dusted and folded it.

"I'm willing she should hear about it," Rebecca answered. "I didn't do anything to be ashamed of! I saw the flag in the back of Mr. Simpson's wagon and I just followed it. There weren't any men or any Dorcases to take care of it and so it fell to me! You wouldn't have had me let it out of my sight, would you, and we going to raise it tomorrow morning?"

"Rebecca's perfectly right, Mrs. Meserve!" said Miss Dearborn proudly. "And it's lucky there was somebody quick-witted enough to ride and consort' with Mr. Simpson! I don't know what the village will think, but seems to me the town clerk might write down in his book, *This day the State of Maine saved the flag!*"

I

The foregoing episode, if narrated in a romance, would undoubtedly have been called "The Saving of the Colors," but at the nightly conversazione in Watson's store it was alluded to as the way little Becky Randall got the flag away from Slippery Simpson.

Dramatic as it was, it passed into the limbo of half-forgotten things in Rebecca's mind, its brief importance submerged in the glories of the next day.

There was a painful prelude to these glories. Alice Robinson came to spend the night with Rebecca, and when the bedroom door closed upon the two girls, Alice announced here intention of "doing up" Rebecca's front hair in leads and rags, and braiding the back in six tight, wetted braids.

Rebecca demurred. Alice persisted.

"Your hair is so long and thick and dark and straight," she said, "that you'll look like an Injun!"

"I am the State of Maine; it all belonged to the Indians once," Rebecca remarked gloomily, for she was curiously shy about discussing her personal appearance.

"And your wreath of little pine-cones won't set decent without crimps," continued Alice.

Rebecca glanced in the cracked looking-glass and met what she considered an accusing lack of beauty, a sight that always either saddened or enraged her according to circumstances; then she sat down resignedly and began to help Alice in the philanthropic work of making the State of Maine fit to be seen at the raising.

Neither of the girls was an expert hairdresser, and at the end of an hour, when the sixth braid was tied, and Rebecca had given one last shuddering look in the mirror, both were ready to weep with fatigue.

The candle was blown out and Alice soon went to sleep, but Rebecca tossed on her pillow, its goose-feathered softness all dented by the cruel lead knobs and the knots of twisted rags. She slipped out of bed and walked to and fro, holding her aching head with both hands. Finally she leaned on the window-sill, watching the still weather-vane on Alice's barn and breathing in the fragrance of the ripening apples, until her restlessness subsided under the clear starry beauty of the night.

At six in the morning the girls were out of bed, for Alice could hardly wait until Rebecca's hair was taken down, she was so eager to see the result of her labors.

The leads and rags were painfully removed, together with much hair, the operation being punctuated by a series of squeaks, squeals, and shrieks on the part of Rebecca and a series of warnings from Alice, who wished the preliminaries to be kept secret from the aunts, that they might the more fully appreciate the radiant result.

Then came the unbraiding, and then—dramatic moment—the "combing out;" a difficult, not to say impossible process, in which the hairs that had resisted the earlier stages almost gave up the ghost.

The long front strands had been wound up from various angles and by various methods, so that, when released, they assumed the strangest, most obstinate, most unexpected attitudes. When the comb was dragged through the last braid, the wild, tortured, electric hairs following, and then rebounding from it in a bristling, snarling tangle. Massachusetts gave one encompassing glance at the State o' Maine's head, and announced her intention of going home to breakfast! She was deeply grieved at the result of her attempted beautifying, but she felt that meeting Miss Miranda Sawyer at the morning meal would not mend matters in the least, so slipping out of the side door, she ran up Guide Board hill as fast as her legs could carry her.

The State o' Maine, deserted and somewhat unnerved, sat down before the glass and attacked her hair doggedly and with set lips, working over it until Miss Jane called her to breakfast; then, with a boldness born of despair, she entered the dining room, where her aunts were already seated at table. To "draw fire" she whistled, a forbidden joy, which only attracted more attention, instead of diverting it. There was a moment of silence after the grotesque figure was fully taken in; then came a moan from Jane and a groan from Miranda.

"What have you done to yourself?" asked Miranda sternly.

"Made an effort to be beautiful and failed!" jauntily replied Rebecca, but she was too miserable to keep up the fiction. "Oh, Aunt Miranda, don't scold. I'm so unhappy! Alice and I rolled up my hair to curl it for the raising. She said it was so straight I looked like an Indian!"

"Mebbe you did," vigorously agreed Miranda, "but 't any rate you looked like a Christian Injun, 'n' now you look like a heathen Injun; that's all the difference I can see. What can we do with her, Jane, between this and nine o'clock?"

"We'll all go out to the pump just as soon as we're through breakfast," answered Jane soothingly. "We can accomplish consid'rable with water and force."

Rebecca nibbled her corn-cake, her tearful eyes cast on her plate and her chin quivering.

"Don't you cry and red your eyes up," chided Miranda quite kindly; "the minute you've eat enough run up and get your brush and comb and meet us at the back door."

"I wouldn't care myself how bad I looked," said Rebecca, "but I can't bear to be so homely that I shame the State of Maine!"

Oh, what an hour followed this plaint! Did any aspirant for literary or dramatic honors ever pass to fame through such an antechamber of horrors? Did poet of the day ever have his head so maltreated? To be dipped in the rain-water tub, soused again and again; to be held under the spout and pumped on; to be rubbed furiously with rough roller towels; to be dried with hot flannels! And is it not well-nigh incredible that at the close of such an hour the ends of the long hair should still stand out straight, the braids having been turned up two inches by Alice, and tied hard in that position with linen thread?

"Get out the skirt-board, Jane," cried Miranda, to whom

opposition served as a tonic, "and move that flat-iron on to the front o' the stove. Rebecca, set down in that low chair beside the board, and Jane, you spread out her hair on it and cover it up with brown paper. Don't cringe, Rebecca; the worst's over, and you've borne up real good! I'll be careful not to pull your hair nor scorch you, and oh, HOW I'd like to have Alice Robinson acrost my knee and a good strip o' shingle in my right hand! There, you're all ironed out and your Aunt Jane can put on your white dress and braid your hair up again good and tight. Perhaps you won't be the hombliest of the states, after all; but when I see you comin' in to breakfast I said to myself: I guess if Maine looked like that, it wouldn't never a' been admitted into the Union!'"

When Uncle Sam and the stagecoach drew up to the brick house with a grand swing and a flourish, the goddess of Liberty and most of the States were already in their places on the "harricane deck."

Words fail to describe the gallant bearing of the horses, their headstalls gayly trimmed and their harnesses dotted with little flags. The stage windows were hung in bunting, and from within beamed Columbia, looking out from the bright frame as if proud of her freight of loyal children. Patriotic streamers floated from whip, from dash-board and from rumble, and the effect of the whole was something to stimulate the most phlegmatic voter.

Rebecca came out on the steps and Aunt Jane brought a chair to assist in the ascent. Miss Dearborn peeped from the window, and gave a despairing look at her favorite.

What had happened to her? Who had dressed her? Had her head been put through a wringing-machine? Why were her eyes red and swollen? Miss Dearborn determined to take her behind the trees in the pine grove and give her some finishing touches; touches that her skillful fingers fairly itched to bestow.

The stage started, and as the roadside pageant grew gayer and gayer, Rebecca began to brighten and look prettier, for most of her beautifying came from within. The people, walking, driving, or standing on their doorsteps, cheered Uncle Sam's coach with its freight of gossamer-muslined, fluttering-ribboned girls, and just

99

behind, the gorgeously decorated haycart, driven by Abijah Flagg, bearing the jolly but inharmonious fife-and-drum corps.

Was ever such a golden day! Such crystal air! Such mellow sunshine! Such a merry Uncle Sam!

The stage drew up at an appointed spot near a pine grove, and while the crowd was gathering, the children waited for the hour to arrive when they should march to the platform; the hour toward which they seemed to have been moving since the dawn of creation.

As soon as possible Miss Dearborn whispered to Rebecca: "Come behind the trees with me; I want to make you prettier!"

Rebecca thought she had suffered enough from that process already during the last twelve hours, but she put out an obedient hand and the two withdrew.

Now Miss Dearborn was, I fear, a very indifferent teacher. Dr. Moses always said so, and Libbie Moses, who wanted her school, said it was a pity she hadn't enjoyed more social advantages in her youth. Libbie herself had taken music lessons in Portland; and spent a night at the Profile House in the White Mountains, and had visited her sister in Lowell, Massachusetts. These experiences gave her, in her own mind, and in the mind of her intimate friends, a horizon so boundless that her view of smaller, humbler matters was a trifle distorted.

Miss Dearborn's stock in trade was small, her principal virtues being devotion to children and ability to gain their love, and a power of evolving a schoolroom order so natural, cheery, serene, and peaceful that it gave the beholder a certain sense of being in a district heaven. She was poor in arithmetic and weak in geometry, but if you gave her a rose, a bit of ribbon, and a seven-by-nine looking-glass she could make herself as pretty as a pink in two minutes.

Safely sheltered behind the pines, Miss Dearborn began to practice mysterious feminine arts. She flew at Rebecca's tight braids, opened the strands and rebraided them loosely; bit and tore the red, white, and blue ribbon in two and tied the braids separately. Then with nimble fingers she pulled out little tendrils of hair behind the ears and around the nape of the neck. After a glance

100

of acute disapproval directed at the stiff balloon skirt she knelt on the ground and gave a strenuous embrace to Rebecca's knees, murmuring, between her hugs, "Starch must be cheap at the brick house!"

This particular line of beauty attained, there ensued great pinchings of ruffles, her fingers that could never hold a ferrule nor snap children's ears being incomparable fluting-irons.

Next the sash was scornfully untied and tightened to suggest something resembling a waist. The chastened bows that had been squat, dowdy, spiritless, were given tweaks, flirts, bracing little pokes and dabs, till, acknowledging a master hand, they stood up, piquant, pert, smart, alert!

Pride of bearing was now infused into the flattened lace at the neck, and a pin (removed at some sacrifice from her own toilette) was darned in at the back to prevent any cowardly lapsing. The short white cotton gloves that called attention to the tanned wrist and arms were stripped off and put in her own pocket. Then the wreath of pine-cones was adjusted at a heretofore unimagined angle, the hair was pulled softly into a fluffy frame, and finally, as she met Rebecca's grateful eyes she gave her two approving, triumphant kisses. In a second the sensitive face lighted into happiness; pleased dimples appeared in the cheeks, the kissed mouth was as red as a rose, and the little fright that had walked behind the pine-tree stepped out on the other side Rebecca the lovely.

As to the relative value of Miss Dearborn's accomplishments, the decision must be left to the gentle reader; but though it is certain that children should be properly grounded in mathematics, no heart of flesh could bear to hear Miss Dearborn's methods vilified who had seen her patting, pulling, squeezing Rebecca from ugliness into beauty.

The young superintendent of district schools was a witness of the scene, and when later he noted the children surrounding Columbia as bees a honeysuckle, he observed to Dr. Moses: "She may not be much of a teacher, but I think she'd be considerable of a wife!" and subsequent events proved that he meant what he said!

II

Now all was ready; the moment of fate was absolutely at hand; the fife-and-drum corps led the way and the States followed; but what actually happened Rebecca never knew; she lived through the hours in a waking dream. Every little detail was a facet of light that reflected sparkles, and among them all she was fairly dazzled. The brass band played inspiring strains; the mayor spoke eloquently on great themes; the people cheered; then the rope on which so much depended was put into the children's hands, they applied superhuman strength to their task, and the flag mounted, mounted, smoothly and slowly, and slowly unwound and stretched itself until its splendid size and beauty were revealed against the maples and pines and blue New England sky.

Then after cheers upon cheers and after a patriotic chorus by the church choirs, the State of Maine mounted the platform, vaguely conscious that she was to recite a poem, though for the life of her she could not remember a single word.

"Speak up loud and clear, Rebecky," whispered Uncle Sam in the front row, but she could scarcely hear her own voice when, tremblingly, she began her first line. After that she gathered strength and the poem "said itself," while the dream went on.

She saw Adam Ladd leaning against a tree; Aunt Jane and Aunt Miranda palpitating with nervousness; Clara Belle Simpson gazing cross-eyed but adoring from a seat on the side; and in the far, far distance, on the very outskirts of the crowd, a tall man standing in a wagon—a tall, loose-jointed man with red upturned mustaches, and a gaunt white horse headed toward the Acreville road.

Loud applause greeted the state of Maine, the slender little white-clad figure standing on the mossy boulder that had been used as the centre of the platform. The sun came up from behind a great maple and shone full on the star-spangled banner, making it more dazzling than ever, so that its beauty drew all eyes upward.

Abner Simpson lifted his vagrant shifting gaze to its softy fluttering folds and its splendid massing of colors, thinking:

"I don't know's anybody'd ought to steal a flag—the thunderin'

102

idjuts seem to set such store by it, and what is it, anyway? Nothin; but a sheet o' buntin!"

Nothing but a sheet of bunting? He looked curiously at the rapt faces of the mothers, their babies asleep in their arms; the parted lips and shining eyes of the white-clad girls; at Cap'n Lord, who had been in Libby prison, and Nat Strout, who had left an arm at Bull Run; at the friendly, jostling crowd of farmers, happy, eager, absorbed, their throats ready to burst with cheers. Then the breeze served, and he heard Rebecca's clear voice saying:—

"For it's your star, my star, all the stars together,
That make our country's flag so proud
To float in the bright fall weather!"

"Talk about stars! She's got a couple of em right in her head," thought Simpson.... "If I ever seen a young one like that lyin; on anybody's doorstep I'd hook her quicker'n a wink, though I've got plenty to home, the Lord knows! And I wouldn't swap her off neither.... Spunky little creeter, too; settin; up in the wagon lookin' bout's big as a pint o' cider, but keepin' right after the goods!... I vow I'm bout sick o' my job! Never WITH the crowd, allers JEST on the outside, s if I wa'n't as good's they be! If it paid well, mebbe I wouldn't mind, but they're so thunderin' stingy round here, they don't leave anything decent out for you to take from em, yet you're reskin' your liberty n' reputation jest the same!... Countin' the poor pickin's n' the time I lose in jail I might most's well be done with it n' work out by the day, as the folks want me to; I'd make bout's much n' I don't know's it would be any harder!"

He could see Rebecca stepping down from the platform, while his own red-headed little girl stood up on her bench, waving her hat with one hand, her handkerchief with the other, and stamping with both feet.

Now a man sitting beside the mayor rose from his chair and Abner heard him call:

"Three cheers for the women who made the flag!"

"Hip, hip, hurrah!"

"Three cheers for the State of Maine!"

103

"Hip, hip, hurrah!"

"Three cheers for the girl that saved the flag from the hands of the enemy!"

"Hip, hip, hurrah! Hip, hip, hurrah!"

It was the Edgewood minister, whose full, vibrant voice was of the sort to move a crowd. His words rang out into the clear air and were carried from lip to lip. Hands clapped, feet stamped, hats swung, while the loud huzzahs might almost have wakened the echoes on old Mount Ossipee.

The tall, loose-jointed man sat down in the wagon suddenly and took up the reins.

"They're gettin' a little mite personal, and I guess it's bout time for you to be goin', Simpson!"

The tone was jocular, but the red mustaches drooped, and the half-hearted cut he gave to start the white mare on her homeward journey showed that he was not in his usual devil-may-care mood.

"Durn his skin!" he burst out in a vindictive undertone, as the mare swung into her long gait. "It's a lie! I thought twas somebody's wash! I hain't an enemy!"

While the crowd at the raising dispersed in happy family groups to their picnics in the woods; while the Goddess of Liberty, Uncle Sam, Columbia, and the proud States lunched grandly in the Grange hall with distinguished guests and scarred veterans of two wars, the lonely man drove, and drove, and drove through silent woods and dull, sleepy villages, never alighting to replenish his wardrobe or his stock of swapping material.

At dusk he reached a miserable tumble-down house on the edge of a pond.

The faithful wife with the sad mouth and the habitual look of anxiety in her faded eyes came to the door at the sound of wheels and went doggedly to the horse-shed to help him unharness.

"You didn't expect to see me back tonight, did ye?" he asked satirically; "leastwise not with this same horse? Well, I'm here! You needn't be scairt to look under the wagon seat, there hain't nothin' there, not even my supper, so I hope you're suited for once! No, I guess I hain't goin' to be an angel right away, neither. There wa'n't

104

nothin' but flags layin' roun' loose down Riverboro way, n' whatever they say, I hain't sech a hound as to steal a flag!"

It was natural that young Riverboro should have red, white, and blue dreams on the night after the new flag was raised. A stranger thing, perhaps, is the fact that Abner Simpson should lie down on his hard bed with the flutter of bunting before his eyes, and a whirl of unaccustomed words in his mind.

"For it's your star, my star, all our stars together."

"I'm sick of goin' it alone," he thought; "I guess I'll try the other road for a spell;" and with that he fell asleep.

SEVENTH CHRONICLE

THE LITTLE PROPHET

I

"I guess York County will never get red of that Simpson crew!" exclaimed Miranda Sawyer to Jane. "I thought when the family moved to Acreville we'd seen the last of em, but we ain't! The big, cross-eyed, stutterin' boy has got a place at the mills in Maplewood; that's near enough to come over to Riverboro once in a while of a Sunday mornin' and set in the meetin' house starin' at Rebecca same as he used to do, only it's reskier now both of em are older. Then Mrs. Fogg must go and bring back the biggest girl to help her take care of her baby,—as if there wa'n't plenty of help nearer home! Now I hear say that the youngest twin has come to stop the summer with the Cames up to Edgewood Lower Corner."

"I thought two twins were always the same age," said Rebecca, reflectively, as she came into the kitchen with the milk pail.

"So they be," snapped Miranda, flushing and correcting herself. "But that pasty-faced Simpson twin looks younger and is smaller than the other one. He's meek as Moses and the other one is as bold as a brass kettle; I don't see how they come to be twins; they ain't a mite alike."

"Elijah was always called the fighting twin' at school," said Rebecca, "and Elisha's other name was Nimbi-Pamby; but I think he's a nice little boy, and I'm glad he has come back. He won't like living with Mr. Came, but he'll be almost next door to the minister's, and Mrs. Baxter is sure to let him play in her garden."

"I wonder why the boy's stayin' with Cassius Came," said Jane. "To be sure they haven't got any of their own, but the child's too young to be much use."

"I know why," remarked Rebecca promptly, "for I heard all about it over to Watson's when I was getting the milk. Mr. Came

106

traded something with Mr. Simpson two years ago and got the best of the bargain, and Uncle Jerry says he's the only man that ever did, and he ought to have a monument put up to him. So Mr. Came owes Mr. Simpson money and won't pay it, and Mr. Simpson said he'd send over a child and board part of it out, and take the rest in stock—a pig or a calf or something."

"That's all stuff and nonsense," exclaimed Miranda; "nothin' in the world but store-talk. You git a clump o' men-folks settin' round Watson's stove, or out on the bench at the door, an' they'll make up stories as fast as their tongues can wag. The man don't live that's smart enough to cheat Abner Simpson in a trade, and who ever heard of anybody's owin' him money? Tain't supposable that a woman like Mrs. Came would allow her husband to be in debt to a man like Abner Simpson. It's a sight likelier that she heard that Mrs. Simpson was ailin' and sent for the boy so as to help the family along. She always had Mrs. Simpson to wash for her once a month, if you remember Jane?"

There are some facts so shrouded in obscurity that the most skillful and patient investigator cannot drag them into the light of day. There are also (but only occasionally) certain motives, acts, speeches, lines of conduct, that can never be wholly and satisfactorily explained, even in a village post-office or on the loafers' bench outside the tavern door.

Cassius Came was a close man, close of mouth and close of purse; and all that Riverboro ever knew as to the three months' visit of the Simpson twin was that it actually occurred. Elisha, otherwise Nimbi-Pamby, came; Nimbi-Pamby stayed; and Nimbi-Pamby, when he finally rejoined his own domestic circle, did not go empty-handed (so to speak), for he was accompanied on his homeward travels by a large, red, bony, somewhat truculent cow, who was tied on behind the wagon, and who made the journey a lively and eventful one by her total lack of desire to proceed over the road from Edgewood to Acreville. But that, the cow's tale, belongs to another time and place, and the coward's tale must come first; for Elisha Simpson was held to be sadly lacking in the manly quality of courage.

It was the new minister's wife who called Nimbi-Pamby the

Little Prophet. His full name was Elisha Jeremiah Simpson, but one seldom heard it at full length, since, if he escaped the ignominy of Nimbi-Pamby, Lishe was quite enough for an urchin just in his first trousers and those assumed somewhat prematurely. He was "Lishe," therefore, to the village, but the Little Prophet to the young minister's wife.

Rebecca could see the Cames' brown farmhouse from Mrs. Baxter's sitting-room window. The little-traveled road with strips of tufted green between the wheel tracks curled dustily up to the very doorstep, and inside the screen door of pink mosquito netting was a wonderful drawn-in rug, shaped like a half pie, with "Welcome" in saffron letters on a green ground.

Rebecca liked Mrs. Cassius Came, who was a friend of her Aunt Miranda's and one of the few persons who exchanged calls with that somewhat unsociable lady. The Came farm was not a long walk from the brick house, for Rebecca could go across the fields when haying-time was over, and her delight at being sent on an errand in that direction could not be measured, now that the new minister and his wife had grown to be such a resource in her life. She liked to see Mrs. Came shake the Welcome rug, flinging the cheery word out into the summer sunshine like a bright greeting to the day. She liked to see her go to the screen door a dozen times in a morning, open it a crack and chase an imaginary fly from the sacred precincts within. She liked to see her come up the cellar steps into the side garden, appearing mysteriously as from the bowels of the earth, carrying a shining pan of milk in both hands, and disappearing through the beds of hollyhocks and sunflowers to the pig-pen or the hen-house.

Rebecca was not fond of Mr. Came, and neither was Mrs. Baxter, nor Elisha, for that matter; in fact Mr. Came was rather a difficult person to grow fond of, with his fiery red beard, his freckled skin, and his gruff way of speaking; for there were no children in the brown house to smooth the creases from his forehead or the roughness from his voice.

II

The new minister's wife was sitting under the shade of her great maple early one morning, when she first saw the Little Prophet. A tiny figure came down the grass-grown road leading a cow by a rope. If it had been a small boy and a small cow, a middle-sized boy and an ordinary cow, or a grown man and a big cow, she might not have noticed them; but it was the combination of an infinitesimal boy and a huge cow that attracted her attention. She could not guess the child's years, she only knew that he was small for his age, whatever it was.

The cow was a dark red beast with a crumpled horn, a white star on her forehead, and a large surprised sort of eye. She had, of course, two eyes, and both were surprised, but the left one had an added hint of amazement in it by virtue of a few white hairs lurking accidentally in the centre of the eyebrow.

The boy had a thin sensitive face and curtly brown hair, short trousers patched on both knees, and a ragged straw hat on the back of his head. He pattered along behind the cow, sometimes holding the rope with both hands, and getting over the ground in a jerky way, as the animal left him no time to think of a smooth path for bare feet.

The Came pasture was a good half-mile distant, and the cow seemed in no hurry to reach it; accordingly she forsook the road now and then, and rambled in the hollows, where the grass was sweeter to her way of thinking. She started on one of these exploring expeditions just as she passed the minister's great maple, and gave Mrs. Baxter time to call out to the little fellow, "Is that your cow?"

Elisha blushed and smiled, and tried to speak modestly, but there was a quiver of pride in his voice as he answered suggestively:

"It's—nearly my cow."

"How is that?" asked Mrs. Baxter.

"Why, Mr. Came says when I drive her twenty-nine more times to pasture thout her gettin' her foot over the rope or thout my bein' afraid, she's goin' to be my truly cow. Are you fraid of cows?"

"Ye-e-es," Mrs. Baxter confessed, "I am, just a little. You see, I am nothing but a woman, and boys can't understand how we feel about cows."

"I can! They're awful big things, aren't they?"

"Perfectly enormous! I've always thought a cow coming towards you one of the biggest things in the world."

"Yes; me, too. Don't let's think about it. Do they hook people so very often?"

"No indeed, in fact one scarcely ever hears of such a case."

"If they stepped on your bare foot they'd scrunch it, wouldn't they?"

"Yes, but you are the driver; you mustn't let them do that; you are a free-will boy, and they are nothing but cows."

"I know; but p'raps there is free-will cows, and if they just *would* do it you couldn't help being scrunched, for you mustn't let go of the rope nor run, Mr. Came says.

"No, of course that would never do."

"Where you used to live did all the cows go down into the boggy places when you drove em to pasture, or did some walk in the road?"

"There weren't any cows or any pastures where I used to live; that's what makes me so foolish; why does your cow need a rope?"

"She don't like to go to pasture, Mr. Came says. Sometimes she'd druther stay to home, and so when she gets part way she turns round and comes backwards."

"Dear me!" thought Mrs. Baxter, "what becomes of this boy-mite if the cow has a spell of going backwards?—Do you like to drive her?" she asked.

"N-no, not erzackly; but you see, it'll be my cow if I drive her twenty-nine more times thout her gettin' her foot over the rope and thout my bein' afraid," and a beaming smile gave a transient brightness to his harassed little face. "Will she feed in the ditch much longer?" he asked. "Shall I say Hurrap'? That's what Mr. Came says—*Hurrap*!' like that, and it means to hurry up."

It was rather a feeble warning that he sounded and the cow fed on peacefully. The little fellow looked up at the minister's wife

110

confidingly, and then glanced back at the farm to see if Cassius Came were watching the progress of events.

"What shall we do next?" he asked.

Mrs. Baxter delighted in that warm, cosy little 'WE;' it took her into the firm so pleasantly. She was a weak prop indeed when it came to cows, but all the courage in her soul rose to arms when Elisha said, "What shall WE do next?" She became alert, ingenious, strong, on the instant.

"What is the cow's name?" she asked, sitting up straight in the swing-chair.

"Buttercup; but she don't seem to know it very well. She ain't a mite like a buttercup."

"Never mind; you must shout 'Buttercup!' at the top of your voice, and twitch the rope *hard*; then I'll call, 'Hurrap!' with all my might at the same moment. And if she starts quickly we mustn't run nor seem frightened!"

They did this; it worked to a charm, and Mrs. Baxter looked affectionately after her Little Prophet as the cow pulled him down Tory Hill.

The lovely August days wore on. Rebecca was often at the parsonage and saw Elisha frequently, but Buttercup was seldom present at their interviews, as the boy now drove her to the pasture very early in the morning, the journey thither being one of considerable length and her method of reaching the goal being exceedingly roundabout.

Mr. Came had pointed out the necessity of getting her into the pasture at least a few minutes before she had to be taken out again at night, and though Rebecca didn't like Mr. Came, she saw the common sense of this remark. Sometimes Mrs. Baxter and Rebecca caught a glimpse of the two at sundown, as they returned from the pasture to the twilight milking, Buttercup chewing her peaceful cud, her soft white bag of milk hanging full, her surprised eye rolling in its accustomed "fine frenzy." The frenzied roll did not mean anything, they used to assure Elisha; but if it didn't, it was an awful pity she had to do it, Rebecca thought; and Mrs. Baxter agreed. To have an expression of eye that meant murder, and yet to

111

be a perfectly virtuous and well-meaning animal, this was a calamity indeed.

Mrs. Baxter was looking at the sun one evening as it dropped like a ball of red fire into Wilkins's woods, when the Little Prophet passed.

"It's the twenty-ninth night," he called joyously.

"I am so glad," she answered, for she had often feared some accident might prevent his claiming the promised reward. "Then tomorrow Buttercup will be your own cow?"

"I guess so. That's what Mr. Came said. He's off to Acreville now, but he'll be home tonight, and father's going to send my new hat by him. When Buttercup's my own cow I wish I could change her name and call her Red Rover, but p'r'aps her mother wouldn't like it. When she b'longs to me, mebbe I won't be so fraid of gettin' hooked and scrunched, because she'll know she's mine, and she'll go better. I haven't let her get snarled up in the rope one single time, and I don't show I'm afraid, do I?"

"I should never suspect it for an instant," said Mrs. Baxter encouragingly. "I've often envied you your bold, brave look!"

Elisha appeared distinctly pleased. "I haven't cried, either, when she's dragged me over the pasture bars and peeled my legs. Bill Petes's little brother Charlie says he ain't afraid of anything, not even bears. He says he would walk right up close and cuff em if they dared to yip; but I ain't like that! He ain't scared of elephants or tigers or lions either; he says they're all the same as frogs or chickens to him!"

Rebecca told her Aunt Miranda that evening that it was the Prophet's twenty-ninth night, and that the big red cow was to be his on the morrow.

"Well, I hope it'll turn out that way," she said. "But I ain't a mite sure that Cassius Came will give up that cow when it comes to the point. It won't be the first time he's tried to crawl out of a bargain with folks a good deal bigger than Lisha, for he's terrible close, Cassius is. To be sure he's stiff in his joints and he's glad enough to have a boy to take the cow to the pasture in summer time, but he always has hired help when it comes harvestin'. So Lisha'll be no use from this on; and I dare say the cow is Abner

112

Simpson's anyway. If you want a walk tonight, I wish you'd go up there and ask Mis' Came if she'll lend me an' your Aunt Jane half her yeast-cake. Tell her we'll pay it back when we get ours a Saturday. Don't you want to take Thirza Meserve with you? She's alone as usual while Huldy's entertainin' beaux on the side porch. Don't stay too long at the parsonage!"

III

Rebecca was used to this sort of errand, for the whole village of Riverboro would sometimes be rocked to the very centre of its being by simultaneous desire for a yeast-cake. As the nearest repository was a mile and a half distant, as the yeast-cake was valued at two cents and wouldn't keep, as the demand was uncertain, being dependent entirely on a fluctuating desire for "riz bread," the storekeeper refused to order more than three yeast-cakes a day at his own risk. Sometimes they remained on his hands a dead loss; sometimes eight or ten persons would "hitch up" and drive from distant farms for the coveted article, only to be met with the flat, "No, I'm all out o' yeast-cake; Mis' Simmons took the last; mebbe you can borry half o' hern, she hain't much of a bread-eater."

So Rebecca climbed the hills to Mrs. Came's, knowing that her daily bread depended on the successful issue of the call.

Thirza was barefooted, and tough as her little feet were, the long walk over the stubble fields tired her. When they came within sight of the Came barn, she coaxed Rebecca to take a short cut through the turnips growing in long, beautifully weeded rows.

"You know Mr. Came is awfully cross, Thirza, and can't bear anybody to tread on his crops or touch a tree or a bush that belongs to him. I'm kind of afraid, but come along and mind you step softly in between the rows and hold up your petticoat, so you can't possibly touch the turnip plants. I'll do the same. Skip along fast, because then we won't leave any deep footprints."

The children passed safely and noiselessly along, their pleasure

113

a trifle enhanced by the felt dangers of their progress. Rebecca knew that they were doing no harm, but that did not prevent her hoping to escape the gimlet eye of Mr. Came.

As they neared the outer edge of the turnip patch they paused suddenly, petticoats in air.

A great clump of elderberry bushes hid them from the barn, but from the other side of the clump came the sound of conversation: the timid voice of the Little Prophet and the gruff tones of Cassius Came.

Rebecca was afraid to interrupt, and too honest to wish to overhear. She could only hope the man and the boy would pass on to the house as they talked, so she motioned to the paralyzed Thirza to take two more steps and stand with her behind the elderberry bushes. But no! In a moment they heard Mr. Came drag a stool over beside the grindstone as he said:

"Well, now Elisha Jeremiah, we'll talk about the red cow. You say you've drove her a month, do ye? And the trade between us was that if you could drive her a month, without her getting the rope over her foot and without bein' afraid, you was to have her. That's straight, ain't it?"

The Prophet's face burned with excitement, his gingham shirt rose and fell as if he were breathing hard, but he only nodded assent and said nothing.

"Now," continued Mr. Came, "have you made out to keep the rope from under her feet?"

"She ain't got t-t-tangled up one s-single time," said Elisha, stuttering in his excitement, but looking up with some courage from his bare toes, with which he was assiduously threading the grass.

"So far, so good. Now bout bein' afraid. As you seem so certain of gettin' the cow, I suppose you hain't been a speck scared, hev you? Honor bright, now!"

"I—I—not but just a little mite. I"—

"Hold up a minute. Of course you didn't *say* you was afraid, and didn't *show* you was afraid, and nobody knew you *was* afraid, but that ain't the way we fixed it up. You was to call the cow your'n

114

if you could drive her to the pasture for a month without *bein'* afraid. Own up square now, hev you be'n afraid?"

A long pause, then a faint, "Yes."

"Where's your manners?"

"I mean yes, sir."

"How often? If it hain't be'n too many times mebbe I'll let ye off, though you're a reg'lar girl-boy, and'll be runnin' away from the cat bimeby. Has it be'n—twice?"

"Yes," and the Little Prophet's voice was very faint now, and had a decided tear in it.

"Yes what?"

"Yes, sir."

"Has it be'n four times?"

"Y-es, sir." More heaving of the gingham shirt.

"Well, you *air* a thunderin' coward! How many times? Speak up now."

More digging of the bare toes in the earth, and one premonitory tear drop stealing from under the downcast lids, then,—

"A little, most every day, and you can keep the cow," wailed the Prophet, as he turned abruptly and fled behind the shed, where he flung himself into the green depths of a tansy bed, and gave himself up to unmanly sobs.

Cassius Came gave a sort of shamefaced guffaw at the abrupt departure of the boy, and went on into the house, while Rebecca and Thirza made a stealthy circuit of the barn and a polite and circumspect entrance through the parsonage front gate.

Rebecca told the minister's wife what she could remember of the interview between Cassius Came and Elisha Simpson, and tender-hearted Mrs. Baxter longed to seek and comfort her Little Prophet sobbing in the tansy bed, the brand of coward on his forehead, and what was much worse, the fear in his heart that he deserved it.

Rebecca could hardly be prevented from bearding Mr. Came and openly espousing the cause of Elisha, for she was an impetuous, reckless, valiant creature when a weaker vessel was attacked or threatened unjustly.

Mrs. Baxter acknowledged that Mr. Came had been true, in a way, to his word and bargain, but she confessed that she had never heard of so cruel and hard a bargain since the days of Shylock, and it was all the worse for being made with a child.

Rebecca hurried home, her visit quite spoiled and her errand quite forgotten till she reached the brick house door, where she told her aunts, with her customary picturesqueness of speech, that she would rather eat buttermilk bread till she died than partake of food mixed with one of Mr. Came's yeast-cakes; that it would choke her, even in the shape of good raised bread.

"That's all very fine, Rebecky," said her Aunt Miranda, who had a pin-prick for almost every bubble; "but don't forget there's two other mouths to feed in this house, and you might at least give your aunt and me the privilege of chokin' if we feel to want to!"

IV

Mrs. Baxter finally heard from Mrs. Came, through whom all information was sure to filter if you gave it time, that her husband despised a coward, that he considered Elisha a regular mother's-apron-string boy, and that he was "learnin'" him to be brave.

Bill Peters, the hired man, now drove Buttercup to pasture, though whenever Mr. Came went to Moderation or Bonnie Eagle, as he often did, Mrs. Baxter noticed that Elisha took the hired man's place. She often joined him on these anxious expeditions, and, a like terror in both their souls, they attempted to train the red cow and give her some idea of obedience.

"If she only wouldn't look at us that way we would get along real nicely with her, wouldn't we?" prattled the Prophet, straggling along by her side; "and she is a splendid cow; she gives twenty-one quarts a day, and Mr. Came says it's more'n half cream."

The minister's wife assented to all this, thinking that if Buttercup would give up her habit of turning completely round in the road to roll her eyes and elevate her white-tipped eyebrow, she might indeed be an enjoyable companion; but in her present state of

116

development her society was not agreeable, even did she give sixty-one quarts of milk a day. Furthermore, when Mrs. Baxter discovered that she never did any of these reprehensible things with Bill Peters, she began to believe cows more intelligent creatures than she had supposed them to be, and she was indignant to think Buttercup could count so confidently on the weakness of a small boy and a timid woman.

One evening, when Buttercup was more than usually exasperating, Mrs. Baxter said to the Prophet, who was bracing himself to keep from being pulled into a wayside brook where Buttercup loved to dabble, "Elisha, do you know anything about the superiority of mind over matter?"

No, he didn't, though it was not a fair time to ask the question, for he had sat down in the road to get a better purchase on the rope.

"Well, it doesn't signify. What I mean is that we can die but once, and it is a glorious thing to die for a great principle. Give me that rope. I can pull like an ox in my present frame of mind. You run down on the opposite side of the brook, take that big stick wade right in—you are barefooted,—brandish the stick, and, if necessary, do more than brandish. I would go myself, but it is better she should recognize you as her master, and I am in as much danger as you are, anyway. She may try to hook you, of course, but you must keep waving the stick,—die brandishing, Prophet, that's the idea! She may turn and run for me, in which case I shall run too; but I shall die running, and the minister can bury us under our favorite sweet-apple tree!"

The Prophet's soul was fired by the lovely lady's eloquence. Their spirits mounted simultaneously, and they were flushed with a splendid courage in which death looked a mean and paltry thing compared with vanquishing that cow. She had already stepped into the pool, but the Prophet waded in towards her, moving the alder branch menacingly. She looked up with the familiar roll of the eye that had done her such good service all summer, but she quailed beneath the stern justice and the new valor of the Prophet's gaze.

In that moment perhaps she felt ashamed of the misery she had caused the helpless mite. At any rate, actuated by fear, surprise, or remorse, she turned and walked back into the road without a sign

117

of passion or indignation, leaving the boy and the lady rather disappointed at their easy victory. To be prepared for a violent death and receive not even a scratch made them fear that they might possibly have overestimated the danger.

They were better friends than ever after that, the young minister's wife and the forlorn little boy from Acreville, sent away from home he knew not why, unless it were that there was little to eat there and considerably more at the Cash Cames', as they were called in Edgewood. Cassius was familiarly known as Uncle Cash, partly because there was a disposition in Edgewood to abbreviate all Christian names, and partly because the old man paid cash, and expected to be paid cash, for everything.

The late summer grew into autumn, and the minister's great maple flung a flaming bough of scarlet over Mrs. Baxter's swing-chair. Uncle Cash found Elisha very useful at picking up potatoes and apples, but the boy was going back to his family as soon as the harvesting was over.

One Friday evening Mrs. Baxter and Rebecca, wrapped in shawls and "fascinators," were sitting on Mrs. Came's front steps enjoying the sunset. Rebecca was in a tremulous state of happiness, for she had come directly from the Seminary at Wareham to the parsonage, and as the minister was absent at a church conference, she was to stay the night with Mrs. Baxter and go with her to Portland next day.

They were to go to the Islands, have ice cream for luncheon, ride on a horse-car, and walk by the Longfellow house, a programme that so unsettled Rebecca's never very steady mind that she radiated flashes and sparkles of joy, making Mrs. Baxter wonder if flesh could be translucent, enabling the spirit-fires within to shine through?

Buttercup was being milked on the grassy slope near the shed door. As she walked to the barn, after giving up her pailfuls of yellow milk, she bent her neck and snatched a hasty bite from a pile of turnips lying temptingly near. In her haste she took more of a mouthful than would be considered good manners even among cows, and as she disappeared in the barn door they could see a forest of green tops hanging from her mouth, while she painfully

118

attempted to grind up the mass of stolen material without allowing a single turnip to escape.

It grew dark soon afterward and they went into the house to see Mrs. Came's new lamp lighted for the first time, to examine her last drawn-in rug (a wonderful achievement produced entirely from dyed flannel petticoats), and to hear the doctor's wife play "Oft in the Still Night," on the dulcimer.

As they closed the sitting-room door opening on the piazza facing the barn, the women heard the cow coughing and said to one another: "Buttercup was too greedy, and now she has indigestion."

Elisha always went to bed at sundown, and Uncle Cash had gone to the doctor's to have his hand dressed, for he had hurt it is some way in the threshing-machine. Bill Peters, the hired man, came in presently and asked for him, saying that the cow coughed more and more, and it must be that something was wrong, but he could not get her to open her mouth wide enough for him to see anything. "She'd up an' die ruther 'n obleege anybody, that tarnal, ugly cow would!" he said.

When Uncle Cash had driven into the yard, he came in for a lantern, and went directly out to the barn. After a half-hour or so, in which the little party had forgotten the whole occurrence, he came in again.

"I'm blamed if we ain't goin' to lose that cow," he said. "Come out, will ye, Hannah, and hold the lantern? I can't do anything with my right hand in a sling, and Bill is the stupidest critter in the country."

Everybody went out to the barn accordingly, except the doctor's wife, who ran over to her house to see if her brother Moses had come home from Milltown, and could come and take a hand in the exercises.

Buttercup was in a bad way; there was no doubt of it. Something, one of the turnips, presumably, had lodged in her throat, and would move neither way, despite her attempts to dislodge it. Her breathing was labored, and her eyes bloodshot from straining and choking. Once or twice they succeeded in getting her mouth partly open, but before they could fairly discover the cause of trouble she had wrested her head away.

119

"I can see a little tuft of green sticking straight up in the middle," said Uncle Cash, while Bill Peters and Moses held a lantern on each side of Buttercup's head; "but, land! It's so far down, and such a mite of a thing, I couldn't git it, even if I could use my right hand. S'pose you try, Bill."

Bill hemmed and hawed, and confessed he didn't care to try. Buttercup's grinders were of good size and excellent quality, and he had no fancy for leaving his hand within her jaws. He said he was no good at that kind of work, but that he would help Uncle Cash hold the cow's head; that was just as necessary, and considerable safer.

Moses was more inclined to the service of humanity, and did his best, wrapping his wrist in a cloth, and making desperate but ineffectual dabs at the slippery green turnip-tops in the reluctantly opened throat. But the cow tossed her head and stamped her feet and switched her tail and wriggled from under Bill's hands, so that it seemed altogether impossible to reach the seat of the trouble.

Uncle Cash was in despair, fuming and fretting the more because of his own crippled hand.

"Hitch up, Bill," he said, "and, Hannah, you drive over to Milliken's Mills for the horse-doctor. I know we can git out that turnip if we can hit on the right tools and somebody to manage em right; but we've got to be quick about it or the critter'll choke to death, sure! Your hand's so clumsy, Mose, she thinks her time's come when she feels it in her mouth, and your fingers are so big you can't ketch holt o' that green stuff thout its slippin'!"

"Mine ain't big; let me try," said a timid voice, and turning round, they saw little Elisha Simpson, his trousers pulled on over his night-shirt, his curly hair ruffled, his eyes vague with sleep.

Uncle Cash gave a laugh of good-humored derision. "You— that's afraid to drive a cow to pasture? No, sir; you hain't got sand enough for this job, I guess!"

Buttercup just then gave a worse cough than ever, and her eyes rolled in her head as if she were giving up the ghost.

"I'd rather do it than see her choke to death!" cried the boy, in despair.

"Then, by ginger, you can try it, sonny!" said Uncle Cash.

120

"Now this time we'll tie her head up. Take it slow, and make a good job of it."

Accordingly they pried poor Buttercup's jaws open to put a wooden gag between them, tied her head up, and kept her as still as they could while the women held the lanterns.

"Now, sonny, strip up your sleeve and reach as fur down's you can! Wind your little fingers in among that green stuff stickin' up there that ain't hardly big enough to call green stuff, give it a twist, and pull for all you're worth. Land! What a skinny little pipe stem!"

The Little Prophet had stripped up his sleeve. It was a slender thing, his arm; but he had driven the red cow all summer, borne her tantrums, protected her from the consequences of her own obstinacy, taking (as he thought) a future owner's pride in her splendid flow of milk—grown fond of her, in a word, and now she was choking to death. A skinny little pipe stem is capable of a deal at such a time, and only a slender hand and arm could have done the work.

Elisha trembled with nervousness, but he made a dexterous and dashing entrance into the awful cavern of Buttercup's mouth; descended upon the tiny clump of green spills or spikes, wound his little fingers in among them as firmly as he could, and then gave a long, steady, determined pull with all the strength in this body. That was not so much in itself, to be sure, but he borrowed a good deal more from some reserve quarter, the location of which nobody knows anything about, but upon which everybody draws in time of need.

Such a valiant pull you would never have expected of the Little Prophet. Such a pull it was that, to his own utter amazement, he suddenly found himself lying flat on his back on the barn floor with a very slippery something in his hand, and a fair-sized but rather dilapidated turnip at the end of it.

"That's the business!" cried Moses.

"I could 'a' done it as easy as nothin' if my arm had been a leetle mite smaller," said Bill Peters.

"You're a trump, sonny!" exclaimed Uncle Cash, as he helped Moses untie Buttercup's head and took the gag out.

121

"You're a trump, Lisha, and, by ginger, the cow's your'n; only don't you let your blessed pa drink none of her cream!"

The welcome air rushed into Buttercup's lungs and cooled her parched, torn throat. She was pretty nearly spent, poor thing, and bent her head (rather gently for her) over the Little Prophet's shoulder as he threw his arms joyfully about her neck, and whispered, "You're my truly cow now, ain't you, Buttercup?"

"Mrs. Baxter, dear," said Rebecca, as they walked home to the parsonage together under the young harvest moon; "there are all sorts of cowards, aren't there, and don't you think Elisha is one of the best kind."

"I don't quite know what to think about cowards, Rebecca Rowena," said the minister's wife hesitatingly. "The Little Prophet is the third coward I have known in my short life who turned out to be a hero when the real testing time came. Meanwhile the heroes themselves—or the ones that were taken for heroes—were always busy doing something, or being somewhere, else."

EIGHTH CHRONICLE

ABNER SIMPSON'S NEW LEAF

Rebecca had now cut the bonds that bound her to the Riverboro district school, and had been for a week a full-fledged pupil at the Wareham Seminary, towards which goal she had been speeding ever since the memorable day when she rode into Riverboro on the top of Uncle Jerry Cobb's stagecoach, and told him that education was intended to be "the making of her."

She went to and fro, with Emma Jane and the other Riverboro boys and girls, on the morning and evening trains that ran between the academy town and Milliken's Mills.

The six days had passed like a dream! — a dream in which she sat in corners with her eyes cast down; flushed whenever she was addressed; stammered whenever she answered a question, and nearly died of heart failure when subjected to an examination of any sort. She delighted the committee when reading at sight from "King Lear," but somewhat discouraged them when she could not tell the capital of the United States. She admitted that her former teacher, Miss Dearborn, might have mentioned it, but if so she had not remembered it.

In these first weeks among strangers she passed for nothing but an interesting-looking, timid, innocent, country child, never revealing, even to the far-seeing Emily Maxwell, a hint of her originality, facility, or power in any direction. Rebecca was fourteen, but so slight, and under the paralyzing new conditions so shy, that she would have been mistaken for twelve had it not been for her general advancement in the school curriculum.

Growing up in the solitude of a remote farm house, transplanted to a tiny village where she lived with two elderly spinsters, she was still the veriest child in all but the practical duties and responsibilities of life; in those she had long been a woman.

It was Saturday afternoon; her lessons for Monday were all

learned and she burst into the brick house sitting-room with the flushed face and embarrassed mien that always foreshadowed a request. Requests were more commonly answered in the negative than in the affirmative at the brick house, a fact that accounted for the slight confusion in her demeanor.

"Aunt Miranda," she began, "the fishman says that Clara Belle Simpson wants to see me very much, but Mrs. Fogg can't spare her long at a time, you know, on account of the baby being no better; but Clara Belle could walk a mile up, and I a mile down the road, and we could meet at the pink house half way. Then we could rest and talk an hour or so, and both be back in time for our suppers. I've fed the cat; she had no appetite, as it's only two o'clock and she had her dinner at noon, but she'll go back to her saucer, and it's off my mind. I could go down cellar now and bring up the cookies and the pie and doughnuts for supper before I start. Aunt Jane saw no objection; but we thought I'd better ask you so as to run no risks."

Miranda Sawyer, who had been patiently waiting for the end of this speech, laid down her knitting and raised her eyes with a half-resigned expression that meant: Is there anything unusual in heaven or earth or the waters under the earth that this child does not want to do? Will she ever settle down to plain, comprehensible Sawyer ways, or will she to the end make these sudden and radical propositions, suggesting at every turn the irresponsible Randall ancestry?

"You know well enough, Rebecca, that I don't like you to be intimate with Abner Simpson's young ones," she said decisively. "They ain't fit company for anybody that's got Sawyer blood in their veins, if it's ever so little. I don't know, I'm sure, how you're goin' to turn out! The fish peddler seems to be your best friend, without it's Abijah Flagg that you're everlastingly talkin' to lately. I should think you'd rather read some improvin' book than to be chatterin' with Squire Bean's chore-boy!"

"He isn't always going to be a chore-boy," explained Rebecca, "and that's what we're considering. It's his career we talk about, and he hasn't got any father or mother to advise him. Besides, Clara Belle kind of belongs to the village now that she lives with Mrs.

Fogg; and she was always the best behaved of all the girls, either in school or Sunday-school. Children can't help having fathers!"

"Everybody says Abner is turning over a new leaf, and if so, the family'd ought to be encouraged every possible way," said Miss Jane, entering the room with her mending basket in hand.

"If Abner Simpson is turnin' over a leaf, or anythin' else in creation, it's only to see what's on the under side!" remarked Miss Miranda promptly. "Don't talk to me about new leaves! You can't change that kind of a man; he is what he is, and you can't make him no different!"

"The grace of God can do consid'rable," observed Jane piously.

"I ain't sayin' but it can if it sets out, but it has to begin early and stay late on a man like Simpson."

"Now, Mirandy, Abner ain't more'n forty! I don't know what the average age for repentance is in men-folks, but when you think of what an awful sight of em leaves it to their deathbeds, forty seems real kind of young. Not that I've heard Abner has experienced religion, but everybody's surprised at the good way he's conductin' this fall."

"They'll be surprised the other way round when they come to miss their firewood and apples and potatoes again," affirmed Miranda.

"Clara Belle don't seem to have inherited from her father," Jane ventured again timidly. "No wonder Mrs. Fogg sets such store by the girl. If it hadn't been for her, the baby would have been dead by now."

"Perhaps tryin' to save it was interferin' with the Lord's will," was Miranda's retort.

"Folks can't stop to figure out just what's the Lord's will when a child has upset a kettle of scalding water on to himself," and as she spoke Jane darned more excitedly. "Mrs. Fogg knows well enough she hadn't ought to have left that baby alone in the kitchen with the stove, even if she did see Clara Belle comin' across lots. She'd ought to have waited before drivin' off; but of course she was afraid of missing the train, and she's too good a woman to be held accountable."

"The minister's wife says Clara Belle is a real—I can't think of

125

the word!" chimed in Rebecca. "What's the female of hero? Whatever it is, that's what Mrs. Baxter called her!"

"Clara Belle's the female of Simpson; that's what she is," Miss Miranda asserted; "but she's been brought up to use her wits, and I ain't sayin' but she used em."

"I should say she did!" exclaimed Miss Jane; "to put that screaming, suffering child in the baby-carriage and run all the way to the doctor's when there wasn't a soul on hand to advise her! Two or three more such actions would make the Simpson name sound consid'rable sweeter in this neighborhood."

"Simpson will always sound like Simpson to me!" vouchsafed the elder sister, "but we've talked enough about em an' to spare. You can go along, Rebecca; but remember that a child is known by the company she keeps."

"All right, Aunt Miranda; thank you!" cried Rebecca, leaping from the chair on which she had been twisting nervously for five minutes. "And how does this strike you? Would you be in favor of my taking Clara Belle a company-tart?"

"Don't Mrs. Fogg feed the young one, now she's taken her right into the family?"

"Oh, yes," Rebecca answered, "she has lovely things to eat, and Mrs. Fogg won't even let her drink skim milk; but I always feel that taking a present lets the person know you've been thinking about them and are extra glad to see them. Besides, unless we have company soon, those tarts will have to be eaten by the family, and a new batch made; you remember the one I had when I was rewarding myself last week? That was queer—but nice," she added hastily.

"Mebbe you could think of something of your own you could give away without taking my tarts!" responded Miranda tersely; the joints of her armor having been pierced by the fatally keen tongue of her niece, who had insinuated that company-tarts lasted a long time in the brick house. This was a fact; indeed, the company-tart was so named, not from any idea that it would ever be eaten by guests, but because it was too good for every-day use.

Rebecca's face crimsoned with shame that she had drifted into an impolite and, what was worse, an apparently ungrateful speech.

"I didn't mean to say anything not nice, Aunt Miranda," she stammered. "Truly the tart was splendid, but not exactly like new, that's all. And oh! I know what I can take Clara Belle! A few chocolate drops out of the box Mr. Ladd gave me on my birthday."

"You go down cellar and get that tart, same as I told you," commanded Miranda, "and when you fill it don't uncover a new tumbler of jelly; there's some dried-apple preserves open that'll do. Wear your rubbers and your thick jacket. After runnin' all the way down there—for your legs never seem to be rigged for walkin' like other girls'—you'll set down on some damp stone or other and ketch your death o' cold, an' your Aunt Jane n' I'll be kep' up nights nursin' you and luggin' your meals upstairs to you on a waiter."

Here Miranda leaned her head against the back of her rocking chair, dropped her knitting and closed her eyes wearily, for when the immovable body is opposed by the irresistible force there is a certain amount of jar and disturbance involved in the operation.

Rebecca moved toward the side door, shooting a questioning glance at Aunt Jane as she passed. The look was full of mysterious suggestion and was accompanied by an almost imperceptible gesture. Miss Jane knew that certain articles were kept in the entry closet, and by this time she had become sufficiently expert in telegraphy to know that Rebecca's unspoken query meant: *"Could you permit the hat with the red wings, it being Saturday, fine settled weather, and a pleasure excursion?"*

These confidential requests, though fraught with embarrassment when Miranda was in the room, gave Jane much secret joy; there was something about them that stirred her spinster heart—they were so gay, so appealing, so un-Sawyer-, un-Riverboro-like. The longer Rebecca lived in the brick house the more her Aunt Jane marveled at the child. What made her so different from everybody else. Could it be that her graceless popinjay of a father, Lorenzo de Medici Randall, had bequeathed her some strange combination of gifts instead of fortune? Her eyes, her brows, the color of her lips, the shape of her face, as well as her ways and words, proclaimed her a changeling in the Sawyer tribe; but what an enchanting changeling; bringing wit and nonsense and color and delight into the gray monotony of the dragging years!

127

There was frost in the air, but a bright cheery sun, as Rebecca walked decorously out of the brick house yard. Emma Jane Perkins was away over Sunday on a visit to a cousin in Moderation; Alice Robinson and Candace Milliken were having measles, and Riverboro was very quiet. Still, life was seldom anything but a gay adventure to Rebecca, and she started afresh every morning to its conquest. She was not exacting; the Asmodean feat of spinning a sand heap into twine was, poetically speaking, always in her power, so the mile walk to the pink-house gate, and the tryst with freckled, red-haired Clara Belle Simpson, whose face Miss Miranda said looked like a raw pie in a brick oven, these commonplace incidents were sufficiently exhilarating to brighten her eye and quicken her step.

As the great bare horse-chestnut near the pink-house gate loomed into view, the red linsey-woolsey speck going down the road spied the blue linsey-woolsey speck coming up, and both specks flew over the intervening distance and, meeting, embraced each other ardently, somewhat to the injury of the company-tart.

"Didn't it come out splendidly?" exclaimed Rebecca. "I was so afraid the fishman wouldn't tell you to start exactly at two, or that one of us would walk faster than the other; but we met at the very spot! It was a very uncommon idea, wasn't it? Almost romantic!"

"And what do you think?" asked Clara Belle proudly. "Look at this! Mrs. Fogg lent me her watch to come home by!"

"Oh, Clara Belle, how wonderful! Mrs. Fogg gets kinder and kinder to you, doesn't she? You're not homesick any more, are you?"

"No-o; not really; only when I remember there's only little Susan to manage the twins; though they're getting on real well without me. But I kind of think, Rebecca, that I'm going to be given away to the Foggs for good."

"Do you mean adopted?"

"Yes; I think father's going to sign papers. You see we can't tell how many years it'll be before the poor baby outgrows its burns, and Mrs. Fogg'll never be the same again, and she must have somebody to help her."

"You'll be their real daughter, then, won't you, Clara Belle?

And Mr. Fogg is a deacon, and a selectman, and a road commissioner, and everything splendid."

"Yes; I'll have board, and clothes, and school, and be named Fogg, and" (here her voice sank to an awed whisper) "the upper farm if I should ever get married; Miss Dearborn told me that herself, when she was persuading me not to mind being given away."

"Clara Belle Simpson!" exclaimed Rebecca in a transport. "Who'd have thought you'd be a female hero and an heiress besides? It's just like a book story, and it happened in Riverboro. I'll make Uncle Jerry Cobb allow there CAN be Riverboro stories, you see if I don't."

"Of course I know it's all right," Clara Belle replied soberly. "I'll have a good home and father can't keep us all; but it's kind of dreadful to be given away, like a piano or a horse and carriage!"

Rebecca's hand went out sympathetically to Clara Belle's freckled paw. Suddenly her own face clouded and she whispered:

"I'm not sure, Clara Belle, but I'm given away too—do you s'pose I am? Poor father left us in debt, you see. I thought I came away from Sunnybrook to get an education and then help pay off the mortgage; but mother doesn't say anything about my coming back, and our family's one of those too-big ones, you know, just like yours."

"Did your mother sign papers to your aunts?'

"If she did I never heard anything about it; but there's something pinned on to the mortgage that mother keeps in the drawer of the bookcase."

"You'd know it if twas adoption papers; I guess you're just lent," Clara Belle said cheeringly. "I don't believe anybody'd ever give YOU away! And, oh! Rebecca, father's getting on so well! He works on Daly's farm where they raise lots of horses and cattle, too, and he breaks all the young colts and trains them, and swaps off the poor ones, and drives all over the country. Daly told Mr. Fogg he was splendid with stock, and father says it's just like play. He's sent home money three Saturday nights."

"I'm so glad!" exclaimed Rebecca sympathetically. "Now your mother'll have a good time and a black silk dress, won't she?"

"I don't know," sighed Clara Belle, and her voice was grave. "Ever since I can remember she's just washed and cried and cried and washed. Miss Dearborn has been spending her vacation up to Acreville, you know, and she came yesterday to board next door to Mrs. Fogg's. I heard them talking last night when I was getting the baby to sleep—I couldn't help it, they were so close—and Miss Dearborn said mother doesn't like Acreville; she says nobody takes any notice of her, and they don't give her any more work. Mrs. Fogg said, well, they were dreadful stiff and particular up that way and they liked women to have wedding rings."

"Hasn't your mother got a wedding ring?" asked Rebecca, astonished. "Why, I thought everybody *had* to have them, just as they do sofas and a kitchen stove!"

"I never noticed she didn't have one, but when they spoke I remembered mother's hands washing and wringing, and she doesn't wear one, I know. She hasn't got any jewelry, not even a breast-pin."

Rebecca's tone was somewhat censorious, "your father's been so poor perhaps he couldn't afford breast-pins, but I should have thought he'd have given your mother a wedding ring when they were married; that's the time to do it, right at the very first."

"They didn't have any real church dress-up wedding," explained Clara Belle extenuatingly. "You see the first mother, mine, had the big boys and me, and then she died when we were little. Then after a while this mother came to housekeep, and she stayed, and by and by she was Mrs. Simpson, and Susan and the twins and the baby are hers, and she and father didn't have time for a regular wedding in church. They don't have veils and bridesmaids and refreshments round here like Miss Dearborn's sister did."

"Do they cost a great deal—wedding rings?" asked Rebecca thoughtfully. "They're solid gold, so I s'pose they do. If they were cheap we might buy one. I've got seventy-four cents saved up; how much have you?"

"Fifty-three," Clara Belle responded, in a depressing tone; "and anyway there are no stores nearer than Milltown. We'd have to buy it secretly, for I wouldn't make father angry, or shame his pride,

130

now he's got steady work; and mother would know I had spent all my savings."

Rebecca looked nonplussed. "I declare," she said, "I think the Acreville people must be perfectly horrid not to call on your mother only because she hasn't got any jewelry. You wouldn't dare tell your father what Miss Dearborn heard, so he'd save up and buy the ring?"

"No; I certainly would not!" and Clara Belle's lips closed tightly and decisively.

Rebecca sat quietly for a few moments, then she exclaimed jubilantly: "I know where we could get it! From Mr. Aladdin, and then I needn't tell him who it's for! He's coming to stay over tomorrow with his aunt, and I'll ask him to buy a ring for us in Boston. I won't explain anything, you know; I'll just say I need a wedding ring."

"That would be perfectly lovely," replied Clara Belle, a look of hope dawning in her eyes; "and we can think afterwards how to get it over to mother. Perhaps you could send it to father instead, but I wouldn't dare to do it myself. You won't tell anybody, Rebecca?"

"Cross my heart!" Rebecca exclaimed dramatically; and then with a reproachful look, "you know I couldn't repeat a sacred secret like that! Shall we meet next Saturday afternoon, and I tell you what's happened?—Why, Clara Belle, isn't that Mr. Ladd watering his horse at the foot of the hill this very minute? It is; and he's driven up from Milltown stead of coming on the train from Boston to Edgewood. He's all alone, and I can ride home with him and ask him about the ring right away!"

Clara Belle kissed Rebecca fervently, and started on her homeward walk, while Rebecca waited at the top of the long hill, fluttering her handkerchief as a signal.

"Mr. Aladdin! Mr. Aladdin!" she cried, as the horse and wagon came nearer.

Adam Ladd drew up quickly at the sound of the eager young voice.

"Well, well; here is Rebecca Rowena fluttering along the highroad like a red-winged blackbird! Are you going to fly home, or drive with me?"

131

Rebecca clambered into the carriage, laughing and blushing with delight at his nonsense and with joy at seeing him again.

"Clara Belle and I were just talking about you this minute, and I'm so glad you came this way, for there's something very important to ask you about," she began, rather breathlessly.

"No doubt," laughed Adam Ladd, who had become, in the course of his acquaintance with Rebecca, a sort of high court of appeals; "I hope the premium banquet lamp doesn't smoke as it grows older?"

"Now, Mr. Aladdin, you *will* not remember nicely. Mr. Simpson swapped off the banquet lamp when he was moving the family to Acreville; it's not the lamp at all, but once, when you were here last time, you said you'd make up your mind what you were going to give me for Christmas."

"Well," and "I do remember that much quite nicely."

"Well, is it bought?"

"No, I never buy Christmas presents before Thanksgiving."

"Then, *dear* Mr. Aladdin, would you buy me something different, something that I want to give away, and buy it a little sooner than Christmas?"

"That depends. I don't relish having my Christmas presents given away. I like to have them kept forever in little girls' bureau drawers, all wrapped in pink tissue paper; but explain the matter and perhaps I'll change my mind. What is it you want?"

"I need a wedding ring dreadfully," said Rebecca, "but it's a sacred secret."

Adam Ladd's eyes flashed with surprise and he smiled to himself with pleasure. Had he on his list of acquaintances, he asked himself, a person of any age or sex so altogether irresistible and unique as this child? Then he turned to face her with the merry teasing look that made him so delightful to young people.

"I thought it was perfectly understood between us," he said, "that if you could ever contrive to grow up and I were willing to wait, that I was to ride up to the brick house on my snow white" —

"Coal black," corrected Rebecca, with a sparkling eye and a warning finger.

"Coal black charger; put a golden circlet on your lily white finger, draw you up behind me on my pillion" —

"And Emma Jane, too," Rebecca interrupted.

"I think I didn't mention Emma Jane," argued Mr. Aladdin. "Three on a pillion is very uncomfortable. I think Emma Jane leaps on the back of a prancing chestnut, and we all go off to my castle in the forest."

"Emma Jane never leaps, and she'd be afraid of a prancing chestnut," objected Rebecca.

"Then she shall have a gentle cream-colored pony; but now, without any explanation, you ask me to buy you a wedding ring, which shows plainly that you are planning to ride off on a snow white — I mean coal black — charger with somebody else."

Rebecca dimpled and laughed with joy at the nonsense. In her prosaic world no one but Adam Ladd played the game and answered the fool according to his folly. Nobody else talked delicious fairy-story twaddle but Mr. Aladdin.

"The ring isn't for *me!*" she explained carefully. "You know very well that Emma Jane nor I can't be married till we're through Quackenbos's Grammar, Greenleaf's Arithmetic, and big enough to wear long trails and run a sewing machine. The ring is for a friend."

"Why doesn't the groom give it to his bride himself?"

"Because he's poor and kind of thoughtless, and anyway she isn't a bride any more; she has three step and three other kind of children."

Adam Ladd put the whip back in the socket thoughtfully, and then stooped to tuck in the rug over Rebecca's feet and his own. When he raised his head again he asked: "Why not tell me a little more, Rebecca? I'm safe!"

Rebecca looked at him, feeling his wisdom and strength, and above all his sympathy. Then she said hesitatingly: "You remember I told you all about the Simpsons that day on your aunt's porch when you bought the soap because I told you how the family were always in trouble and how much they needed a banquet lamp? Mr. Simpson, Clara Belle's father, has always been very poor, and not always very good, — a little bit *thievish*, you know — but oh, so pleasant and nice to talk to! And now he's turning over a new leaf.

133

And everybody in Riverboro liked Mrs. Simpson when she came here a stranger, because they were sorry for her and she was so patient, and such a hard worker, and so kind to the children. But where she lives now, though they used to know her when she was a girl, they're not polite to her and don't give her scrubbing and washing; and Clara belle heard our teacher say to Mrs. Fogg that the Acreville people were stiff, and despised her because she didn't wear a wedding ring, like all the rest. And Clara Belle and I thought if they were so mean as that, we'd love to give her one, and then she'd be happier and have more work; and perhaps Mr. Simpson if he gets along better will buy her a breast-pin and earrings, and she'll be fitted out like the others. I know Mrs. Peter Meserve is looked up to by everybody in Edgewood on account of her gold bracelets and moss agate necklace."

Adam turned again to meet the luminous, innocent eyes that glowed under the delicate brows and long lashes, feeling as he had more than once felt before, as if his worldly-wise, grown-up thoughts had been bathed in some purifying spring.

"How shall you send the ring to Mrs. Simpson?" he asked, with interest.

"We haven't settled yet; Clara Belle's afraid to do it, and thinks I could manage better. Will the ring cost much? Because, of course, if it does, I must ask Aunt Jane first. There are things I have to ask Aunt Miranda, and others that belong to Aunt Jane."

"It costs the merest trifle. I'll buy one and bring it to you, and we'll consult about it; but I think as you're great friends with Mr. Simpson you'd better send it to him in a letter, letters being your strong point! It's a present a man ought to give his own wife, but it's worth trying, Rebecca. You and Clara Belle can manage it between you, and I'll stay in the background where nobody will see me."

NINTH CHRONICLE

THE GREEN ISLE

Many a green isle needs must be
In the deep sea of misery,
Or the mariner, worn and wan,
Never thus could voyage on
Day and night and night and day,
Drifting on his weary way.

Shelley

Meantime in these frosty autumn days life was crowded with events in the lonely Simpson house at Acreville.

The tumble-down dwelling stood on the edge of Pliney's Pond; so called because old Colonel Richardson left his lands to be divided in five equal parts, each share to be chosen in turn by one of his five sons, Pliny, the eldest, having priority of choice.

Pliny Richardson, having little taste for farming, and being ardently fond of fishing, rowing, and swimming, acted up to his reputation of being "a little mite odd," and took his whole twenty acres in water—hence Pliny's Pond.

The eldest Simpson boy had been working on a farm in Cumberland County for two years. Samuel, generally dubbed "see-saw," had lately found a humble place in a shingle mill and was partially self-supporting. Clara Belle had been adopted by the Foggs; thus there were only three mouths to fill, the capacious ones of Elijah and Elisha, the twin boys, and of lisping, nine-year-old Susan, the capable houseworker and mother's assistant, for the baby had died during the summer; died of discouragement at having been born into a family unprovided with food or money or love or care, or even with desire for, or appreciation of, babies.

There was no doubt that the erratic father of the house had turned over a new leaf. Exactly when he began, or how, or why, or

135

how long he would continue the praiseworthy process,—in a word whether there would be more leaves turned as the months went on,—Mrs. Simpson did not know, and it is doubtful if any authority lower than that of Mr. Simpson's Maker could have decided the matter. He had stolen articles for swapping purposes for a long time, but had often avoided detection, and always escaped punishment until the last few years. Three fines imposed for small offenses were followed by several arrests and two imprisonments for brief periods, and he found himself wholly out of sympathy with the wages of sin. Sin itself he did not especially mind, but the wages thereof were decidedly unpleasant and irksome to him. He also minded very much the isolated position in the community which had lately become his; for he was a social being and would *almost* rather not steal from a neighbor than have him find it out and cease intercourse! This feeling was working in him and rendering him unaccountably irritable and depressed when he took his daughter over to Riverboro at the time of the great flag-raising.

There are seasons of refreshment, as well as seasons of drought, in the spiritual, as in the natural world, and in some way or other dews and rains of grace fell upon Abner Simpson's heart during that brief journey. Perhaps the giving away of a child that he could not support had made the soil of his heart a little softer and readier for planting than usual; but when he stole the new flag off Mrs. Peter Meserve's doorsteps, under the impression that the cotton-covered bundle contained freshly washed clothes, he unconsciously set certain forces in operation.

It will be remembered that Rebecca saw an inch of red bunting peeping from the back of his wagon, and asked the pleasure of a drive with him. She was no daughter of the regiment, but she proposed to follow the flag. When she diplomatically requested the return of the sacred object which was to be the glory of the "raising" next day, and he thus discovered his mistake, he was furious with himself for having slipped into a disagreeable predicament; and later, when he unexpectedly faced a detachment of Riverboro society at the cross-roads, and met not only their wrath and scorn, but the reproachful, disappointed glance of Rebecca's eyes, he felt degraded as never before.

136

The night at the Centre tavern did not help matters, nor the jolly patriotic meeting of the three villages at the flag-raising next morning. He would have enjoyed being at the head and front of the festive preparations, but as he had cut himself off from all such friendly gatherings, he intended at any rate to sit in his wagon on the very outskirts of the assembled crowd and see some of the gayety; for, heaven knows, he had little enough, he who loved talk, and song, and story, and laughter, and excitement.

The flag was raised, the crowd cheered, the little girl to whom he had lied, the girl who was impersonating the State of Maine, was on the platform "speaking her piece," and he could just distinguish some of the words she was saying: —

"For it's your star, my star, all the stars together,
That makes our country's flag so proud
To float in the bright fall weather."

Then suddenly there was a clarion voice cleaving the air, and he saw a tall man standing in the centre of the stage and heard him crying: *"Three cheers for the girl that saved the flag from the hands of the enemy!"*

He was sore and bitter enough already; lonely, isolated enough; with no lot nor share in the honest community life; no hand to shake, no neighbor's meal to share; and this unexpected public arraignment smote him between the eyes. With resentment newly kindled, pride wounded, vanity bleeding, he flung a curse at the joyous throng and drove toward home, the home where he would find his ragged children and meet the timid eyes of a woman who had been the loyal partner of his poverty and disgraces.

It is probable that even then his (extremely light) hand was already on the "new leaf." The angels, doubtless, were not especially proud of the matter and manner of his reformation, but I dare say they were glad to count him theirs on any terms, so difficult is the reformation of this blind and foolish world! They must have been; for they immediately flung into his very lap a profitable, and what is more to the point, an interesting and agreeable situation where money could be earned by doing the very

137

things his nature craved. There were feats of daring to be performed in sight of admiring and applauding stable boys; the horses he loved were his companions; he was *obliged* to "swap," for Daly, his employer, counted on him to get rid of all undesirable stock; power and responsibility of a sort were given him freely, for Daly was no Puritan, and felt himself amply capable of managing any number of Simpsons; so here were numberless advantages within the man's grasp, and wages besides!

Abner positively felt no temptation to steal; his soul expanded with pride, and the admiration and astonishment with which he regarded his virtuous present was only equaled by the disgust with which he contemplated his past; not so much a vicious past, in his own generous estimation of it, as a "thunderin' foolish" one.

Mrs. Simpson took the same view of Abner's new leaf as the angels. She was thankful for even a brief season of honesty coupled with the Saturday night remittance; and if she still washed and cried and cried and washed, as Clara Belle had always seen her, it was either because of some hidden sorrow, or because her poor strength seemed all at once to have deserted her.

Just when employment and good fortune had come to the step-children, and her own were better fed and clothed than ever before, the pain that had always lurked, constant but dull, near her tired heart, grew fierce and triumphantly strong; clutching her in its talons, biting, gnawing, worrying, leaving her each week with slighter powers of resistance. Still hope was in the air and a greater content than had ever been hers was in her eyes; a content that came near to happiness when the doctor ordered her to keep her bed and sent for Clara Belle. She could not wash any longer, but there was the ever new miracle of the Saturday night remittance for household expenses.

"Is your pain bad today, mother," asked Clara Belle, who, only lately given away, was merely borrowed from Mrs. Fogg for what was thought to be a brief emergency.

"Well, there, I can't hardly tell, Clara Belle," Mrs. Simpson replied, with a faint smile. "I can't seem to remember the pain these days without it's extra bad. The neighbors are so kind; Mrs. Little has sent me canned mustard greens, and Mrs. Benson chocolate ice

138

cream and mince pie; there's the doctor's drops to make me sleep, and these blankets and that great box of eatables from Mr. Ladd; and you here to keep me comp'ny! I declare I'm kind o' dazed with comforts. I never expected to see sherry wine in this house. I ain't never drawed the cork; it does me good enough jest to look at Mr. Ladd's bottle settin' on the mantel-piece with the fire shinin' on the brown glass."

Mr. Simpson had come to see his wife and had met the doctor just as he was leaving the house.

"She looks awful bad to me. Is she goin' to pull through all right, same as the last time?" he asked the doctor nervously.

"She's going to pull right through into the other world," the doctor answered bluntly; "and as there don't seem to be anybody else to take the bull by the horns, I'd advise you, having made the woman's life about as hard and miserable as you could, to try and help her to die easy!"

Abner, surprised and crushed by the weight of this verbal chastisement, sat down on the doorstep, his head in his hands, and thought a while solemnly. Thought was not an operation he was wont to indulge in, and when he opened the gate a few minutes later and walked slowly toward the barn for his horse, he looked pale and unnerved. It is uncommonly startling, first to see yourself in another man's scornful eyes, and then, clearly, in your own.

Two days later he came again, and this time it was decreed that he should find Parson Carll tying his piebald mare at the post.

Clara Belle's quick eye had observed the minister as he alighted from his buggy, and, warning her mother, she hastily smoothed the bedclothes, arranged the medicine bottles, and swept the hearth.

"Oh! Don't let him in!" wailed Mrs. Simpson, all of a flutter at the prospect of such a visitor. "Oh, dear! They must think over to the village that I'm dreadful sick, or the minister wouldn't never think of callin'! Don't let him in, Clara Belle! I'm afraid he will say hard words to me, or pray to me; and I ain't never been prayed to since I was a child! Is his wife with him?"

"No; he's alone; but father's just drove up and is hitching at the shed door."

"That's worse than all!" and Mrs. Simpson raised herself feebly

139

on her pillows and clasped her hands in despair. "You mustn't let them two meet, Clara Belle, and you must send Mr. Carll away; your father wouldn't have a minister in the house, nor speak to one, for a thousand dollars!"

"Be quiet, mother! Lie down! It'll be all right! You'll only fret yourself into a spell! The minister's just a good man; he won't say anything to frighten you. Father's talking with him real pleasant, and pointing the way to the front door."

The parson knocked and was admitted by the excited Clara Belle, who ushered him tremblingly into the sickroom, and then betook herself to the kitchen with the children, as he gently requested her.

Abner Simpson, left alone in the shed, fumbled in his vest pocket and took out an envelope which held a sheet of paper and a tiny packet wrapped in tissue paper. The letter had been read once before and ran as follows:

Dear Mr. Simpson:

This is a secret letter. I heard that the Acreville people weren't nice to Mrs. Simpson because she didn't have any wedding ring like all the others.

I know you've always been poor, dear Mr. Simpson, and troubled with a large family like ours at the farm; but you really ought to have given Mrs. Simpson a ring when you were married to her, right at the very first; for then it would have been over and done with, as they are solid gold and last forever. And probably she wouldn't feel like asking you for one, because ladies are just like girls, only grown up, and I know I'd be ashamed to beg for jewelry when just board and clothes cost so much. So I send you a nice, new wedding ring to save your buying, thinking you might get Mrs. Simpson a bracelet or eardrops for Christmas. It did not cost me anything, as it was a secret present from a friend.

I hear Mrs. Simpson is sick, and it would be a great comfort to her while she is in bed and has so much time to look at it. When I had the measles Emma Jane Perkins lent me her mother's garnet ring, and it helped me very much to put my wasted hand outside the bedclothes and see the ring sparkling.

Please don't be angry with me, dear Mr. Simpson, because I

140

like you so much and am so glad you are happy with the horses and colts; and I believe now perhaps you *did* think the flag was a bundle of washing when you took it that day; so no more from your

Trusted friend,
Rebecca Rowena Randall.

Simpson tore the letter slowly and quietly into fragments and scattered the bits on the woodpile, took off his hat, and smoothed his hair; pulled his mustaches thoughtfully, straightened his shoulders, and then, holding the tiny packet in the palm of his hand, he went round to the front door, and having entered the house stood outside the sickroom for an instant, turned the knob and walked softly in.

Then at last the angels might have enjoyed a moment of unmixed joy, for in that brief walk from shed to house Abner Simpson's conscience waked to life and attained sufficient strength to prick and sting, to provoke remorse, to incite penitence, to do all sorts of divine and beautiful things it was meant for, but had never been allowed to do.

Clara Belle went about the kitchen quietly, making preparations for the children's supper. She had left Riverboro in haste, as the change for the worse in Mrs. Simpson had been very sudden, but since she had come she had thought more than once of the wedding ring. She had wondered whether Mr. Ladd had bought it for Rebecca, and whether Rebecca would find means to send it to Acreville; but her cares had been so many and varied that the subject had now finally retired to the background of her mind.

The hands of the clock crept on and she kept hushing the strident tones of Elijah and Elisha, opening and shutting the oven door to look at the corn bread, advising Susan as to her dishes, and marveling that the minister stayed so long.

At last she heard a door open and close and saw the old parson come out, wiping his spectacles, and step into the buggy for his drive to the village.

Then there was another period of suspense, during which the house was as silent as the grave, and presently her father came into

141

the kitchen, greeted the twins and Susan, and said to Clara Belle: "Don't go in there yet!" jerking his thumb towards Mrs. Simpson's room; "she's all beat out and she's just droppin' off to sleep. I'll send some groceries up from the store as I go along. Is the doctor makin' a second call tonight?"

"Yes; he'll be here pretty soon, now," Clara Belle answered, looking at the clock.

"All right. I'll be here again tomorrow, soon as it's light, and if she ain't picked up any I'll send word back to Daly, and stop here with you for a spell till she's better."

It was true; Mrs. Simpson was "all beat out." It had been a time of excitement and stress, and the poor, fluttered creature was dropping off into the strangest sleep—a sleep made up of waking dreams. The pain, that had encompassed her heart like a band of steel, lessened its cruel pressure, and finally left her so completely that she seemed to see it floating above her head; only that it looked no longer like a band of steel, but a golden circle.

The frail bark in which she had sailed her life voyage had been rocking on a rough and tossing ocean, and now it floated, floated slowly into smoother waters.

As long as she could remember, her boat had been flung about in storm and tempest, lashed by angry winds, borne against rocks, beaten, torn, buffeted. Now the waves had subsided; the sky was clear; the sea was warm and tranquil; the sunshine dried the tattered sails; the air was soft and balmy.

And now, for sleep plays strange tricks, the bark disappeared from the dream, and it was she, herself, who was floating, floating farther and farther away; whither she neither knew nor cared; it was enough to be at rest, lulled by the lapping of the cool waves.

Then there appeared a green isle rising from the sea; an isle so radiant and fairy-like that her famished eyes could hardly believe its reality; but it was real, for she sailed nearer and nearer to its shores, and at last her feet skimmed the shining sands and she floated through the air as disembodied spirits float, till she sank softly at the foot of a spreading tree.

Then she saw the green isle was a flowering isle. Every shrub and bush was blooming; the trees were hung with rosy garlands, and even the earth was carpeted with tiny flowers. The rare fragrances, the bird songs, soft and musical, the ravishment of color, all bore down upon her swimming senses at once, taking them captive so completely that she remembered no past, was conscious of no present, looked forward to no future. She seemed to leave the body and the sad, heavy things of the body. The humming in her ears ceased, the light faded, the birds songs grew fainter and more distant, the golden circle of pain receded farther and farther until it was lost to view; even the flowering island gently drifted away, and all was peace and silence.

It was time for the doctor now, and Clara Belle, too anxious to wait longer, softly turned the knob of her mother's door and entered the room. The glow of the open fire illumined the darkest side of the poor chamber. There were no trees near the house, and a full November moon streamed in at the unblinded, uncurtained windows, lighting up the bare interior—the unpainted floor, the gray plastered walls, and the white counterpane.

Her mother lay quite still, her head turned and drooping a little on the pillow. Her left hand was folded softly up against her breast, the fingers of the right partly covering it, as if protecting something precious.

Was it the moonlight that made the patient brow so white, and where were the lines of anxiety and pain? The face of the mother who had washed and cried and cried and washed was as radiant as if the closed eye were beholding heavenly visions.

"Something must have cured her!" thought Clara Belle, awed and almost frightened by the whiteness and the silence.

She tiptoed across the floor to look more closely at the still, smiling shape, and bending over it saw, under the shadow of the caressing right hand, a narrow gold band gleaming on the work-stained finger.

"Oh, the ring came, after all!" she said in a glad whisper, "and perhaps it was that that made her better!"

She put her hand on her mother's gently. A terrified shiver, a warning shudder, shook the girl from head to foot at the chilling touch. A dread presence she had never met before suddenly took shape. It filled the room; stifled the cry on her lips; froze her steps to the floor, stopped the beating of her heart.

Just then the door opened.

"Oh, doctor! Come quick!" she sobbed, stretching out her hand for help, and then covering her eyes. "Come close! Look at mother! Is she better—or is she dead?"

The doctor put one hand on the shoulder of the shrinking child, and touched the woman with the other.

"She is better!" he said gently, "and she is dead."

TENTH CHRONICLE

REBECCA'S REMINISCENCES

Rebecca was sitting by the window in her room at the Wareham Female Seminary. She was alone, as her roommate, Emma Jane Perkins, was reciting Latin down below in some academic vault of the old brick building.

A new and most ardent passion for the classics had been born in Emma Jane's hitherto unfertile brain, for Abijah Flagg, who was carrying off all the prizes at Limerick Academy, had written her a letter in Latin, a letter which she had been unable to translate for herself, even with the aid of a dictionary, and which she had been apparently unwilling that Rebecca, her bosom friend, confidant, and roommate, should render into English.

An old-fashioned Female Seminary, with its allotment of one medium-sized room to two medium sized young females, gave small opportunities for privacy by night or day, for neither the double washstand, nor the thus far unimagined bathroom, nor even indeed the humble and serviceable screen, had been realized, in these dark ages of which I write. Accordingly, like the irrational ostrich, which defends itself by the simple process of not looking at its pursuers, Emma Jane had kept her Latin letter in her closed hand, in her pocket, or in her open book, flattering herself that no one had noticed her pleased bewilderment at its only half-imagined contents.

All the fairies were not present at Rebecca's cradle. A goodly number of them telegraphed that they were previously engaged or unavoidably absent from town. The village of Temperance, Maine, where Rebecca first saw the light, was hardly a place on its own merits to attract large throngs of fairies. But one dear old personage who keeps her pocket full of Merry Leaves from the Laughing Tree, took a fancy to come to the little birthday party; and seeing so few of her sister-fairies present, she dowered the sleeping baby more richly than was her wont, because of its apparent lack of wealth in other directions. So the child grew, and the Merry Leaves from the Laughing Tree rustled where they hung from the hood of her cradle, and, being fairy leaves, when the cradle was given up they festooned themselves on the cribside, and later on blew themselves up to the ceilings at Sunnybook Farm and dangled there, making fun for everybody. They never withered, even at the brick house in Riverboro, where the air was particularly inimical to fairies, for Miss Miranda Sawyer would have scared any ordinary elf out of her seventeen senses. They followed Rebecca to Wareham, and during Abijah Flagg's Latin correspondence with Emma Jane they fluttered about that young person's head in such a manner that Rebecca was almost afraid that she would discover them herself, although this is something, as a matter of fact, that never does happen.

A week had gone by since the Latin missive had been taken from the post-office by Emma Jane, and now, by means of much midnight oil-burning, by much cautious questioning of Miss Maxwell, by such scrutiny of the moods and tenses of Latin verbs as wellnigh destroyed her brain tissue, she had mastered its romantic message. If it was conventional in style, Emma Jane never suspected it. If some of the similes seemed to have been culled from the Latin poets, and some of the phrases built up from Latin exercises, Emma Jane was neither scholar nor critic; the similes, the phrases, the sentiments, when finally translated and written down in black-and-white English, made, in her opinion, the most convincing and heart-melting document ever sent through the mails: —

Mea cara Emma:

Cur audeo scribere ad te epistulam? Es mihi dea! Semper es in mea anima. Iterum et iterum es cum me in somnis. Saepe video tuas capillos auri, tuos pulchros oculos similes caelo, tuas genas, quasi rubentes rosas in nive. Tua vox est dulcior quam cantus avium aut murmur rivuli in montibus.

Cur sum ego tam miser et pauper et indignus, et tu tam dulcis et bona et nobilis?

Si cogitabis de me ero beatus. Tu es sola puella quam amo, et semper eris. Alias puellas non amavi. Forte olim amabis me, sed sum indignus. Sine te sum miser, cum tu es prope mea vita omni est goddamn.

Vale, carissima, carissima puella!
De tuo fideli servo
A. F.

My dear Emma:

Why dare I write to you a letter? You are to me a goddess! Always you are in my heart. Again and again you are with me in dreams. Often I see your locks of gold, your beautiful eyes like the sky, your cheeks, as red roses in snow. Your voice is sweeter than the singing of birds or the murmur of the stream in the mountains.

Why am I so wretched and poor and unworthy, and you so sweet and good and noble?

If you will think of me I shall be happy. You are the only girl that I love and always will be. Other girls I have not loved. Perhaps sometime you will love me, but I am unworthy. Without you, I am wretched, when you are near my life is all joy.

Farewell, dearest, dearest girl!
From your faithful slave
A.F.

Emma Jane knew the letter by heart in English. She even knew it in Latin, only a few days before a dead language to her, but now one filled with life and meaning. From beginning to end the epistle had the effect upon her as of an intoxicating elixir. Often, at morning prayers, or while eating her rice pudding at the noon dinner, or when sinking off to sleep at night, she heard a voice murmuring in her ear, "Vale, carissima, carissima puella!" As to the effect on her modest, countrified little heart of the phrases in which Abijah stated she was a goddess and he her faithful slave, that quite

147

baffles description; for it lifted her bodily out of the scenes in which she moved, into a new, rosy, ethereal atmosphere in which even Rebecca had no place.

Rebecca did not know this, fortunately; she only suspected, and waited for the day when Emma Jane would pour out her confidences, as she always did, and always would until the end of time. At the present moment she was busily employed in thinking about her own affairs. A shabby composition book with mottled board covers lay open on the table before her, and sometimes she wrote in it with feverish haste and absorption, and sometimes she rested her chin in the cup of her palm, and with the pencil poised in the other hand looked dreamily out on the village, its huddle of roofs and steeples all blurred into positive beauty by the fast-falling snowflakes.

It was the middle of December and the friendly sky was softly dropping a great white mantle of peace and good-will over the little town, making all ready within and without for the Feast o' the Babe.

The main street, that in summer was made dignified by its splendid avenue of shade trees, now ran quiet and white between rows of stalwart trunks, whose leafless branches were all hanging heavy under their dazzling burden.

The path leading straight up the hill to the Academy was broken only by the feet of the hurrying, breathless boys and girls who ran up and down, carrying piles of books under their arms; books which they remembered so long as they were within the four walls of the recitation room, and which they eagerly forgot as soon as they met one another in the living, laughing world, going up and down the hill.

"It's very becoming to the universe, snow is!" thought Rebecca, looking out of the window dreamily. "Really there's little to choose between the world and heaven when a snowstorm is going on. I feel as if I ought to look at it every minute. I wish I could get over being greedy, but it still seems to me at sixteen as if there weren't waking hours enough in the day, and as if somehow I were pressed for time and continually losing something. How well I remember mother's story about me when I was four. It was at early breakfast

148

on the farm, but I called all meals dinner' then, and when I had finished I folded up my bib and sighed: O, dear! Only two more dinners, play a while and go to bed!' This was at six in the morning—lamplight in the kitchen, snowlight outside!

> Powdery, powdery, powdery snow,
> Making things lovely wherever you go!
> Merciful, merciful, merciful snow,
> Masking the ugliness hidden below.

Herbert made me promise to do a poem for the January 'Pilot,' but I mustn't take the snow as a subject; there has been too great competition among the older poets!" And with that she turned in her chair and began writing again in the shabby book, which was already three quarters filled with childish scribblings, sometimes in pencil, and sometimes in violet ink with carefully shaded capital letters."

. . . .

Squire Bean has had a sharp attack of rheumatism and Abijah Flagg came back from Limerick for a few days to nurse him. One morning the Burnham sisters from North Riverboro came over to spend the day with Aunt Miranda, and Abijah went down to put up their horse. ("'Commodatin' 'Bijah" was his pet name when we were all young.)

He scaled the ladder to the barn chamber—the dear old ladder that used to be my safety valve!—and pitched down the last forkful of grandfather's hay that will ever be eaten by any visiting horse. They WILL be delighted to hear that it is all gone; they have grumbled at it for years and years.

What should Abijah find at the bottom of the heap but my Thought Book, hidden there two or three years ago and forgotten!

When I think of what it was to me, the place it filled in my life, the affection I lavished on it, I wonder that I could forget it, even in all the excitement of coming to Wareham to school. And that gives me "an uncommon thought" as I used to say! It is this: that when

149

we finish building an air castle we seldom live in it after all; we sometimes even forget that we ever longed to! Perhaps we have gone so far as to begin another castle on a higher hilltop, and this is so beautiful,—especially while we are building, and before we live in it!—that the first one has quite vanished from sight and mind, like the outgrown shell of the nautilus that he casts off on the shore and never looks at again. (At least I suppose he doesn't; but perhaps he takes one backward glance, half-smiling, half-serious, just as I am doing at my old Thought Book, and says, *"Was that my shell! Goodness gracious! how did I ever squeeze myself Into It!"*)

That bit about the nautilus sounds like an extract from a school theme, or a "Pilot" editorial, or a fragment of one of dear Miss Maxwell's lectures, but I think girls of sixteen are principally imitations of the people and things they love and admire; and between editing the "Pilot," writing out Virgil translations, searching for composition subjects, and studying rhetorical models, there is very little of the original Rebecca Rowena about me at the present moment; I am just a member of the graduating class in good and regular standing. We do our hair alike, dress alike as much as possible, eat and drink alike, talk alike,—I am not even sure that we do not think alike; and what will become of the poor world when we are all let loose upon it on the same day of June? Will life, real life, bring our true selves back to us? Will love and duty and sorrow and trouble and work finally wear off the "school stamp" that has been pressed upon all of us until we look like rows of shining copper cents fresh from the mint?

Yet there must be a little difference between us somewhere, or why does Abijah Flagg write Latin letters to Emma Jane, instead of to me? There is one example on the other side of the argument,—Abijah Flagg. He stands out from all the rest of the boys like the Rock of Gibraltar in the geography pictures. Is it because he never went to school until he was sixteen? He almost died of longing to go, and the longing seemed to teach him more than going. He knew his letters, and could read simple things, but it was I who taught him what books really meant when I was eleven and he thirteen. We studied while he was husking corn or cutting potatoes for seed, or shelling beans in the Squire's barn. His beloved Emma Jane didn't teach him; her father wold not have let her be friends with a chore-boy! It was I who found him after milking-time, summer nights, suffering, yes dying, of Least Common Multiple and Greatest Common Divisor; I who struck the shackles from the slave and told him to skip it all and go on to something easier, like Fractions, Percentage, and Compound Interest, as I did myself. Oh! How he used to smell of the cows when I was correcting his sums on warm evenings, but I don't regret it, for he is now the joy of Limerick and the pride of Riverboro, and I suppose has forgotten the proper side on which to approach a cow if you wish to milk her. This now unserviceable knowledge is neatly inclosed in the outgrown shell he threw off two or three years ago. His gratitude to me knows no bounds, but—he writes Latin letters to Emma Jane! But as Mr. Perkins said about drowning the kittens (I now quote from myself at thirteen), "It is the way of the world and how things have to be!"

Well, I have read the Thought Book all through, and when I want to make Mr. Aladdin laugh, I shall show him my composition on the relative values of punishment and reward as builders of character.

I am not at all the same Rebecca today at sixteen that I was then, at twelve and thirteen. I hope, in getting rid of my failings, that I haven't scrubbed and rubbed so hard that I have taken the gloss off the poor little virtues that lay just alongside of the faults; for as I read the foolish doggerel and the funny, funny "Remerniscences," I see on the whole a nice, well-meaning, trusting, loving heedless little creature, that after all I'd rather build on than outgrow altogether, because she is Me; the Me that was made and born just a little different from all the rest of the babies in my birthday year.

One thing is alike in the child and the girl. They both love to set thoughts down in black and white; to see how they look, how they sound, and how they make one feel when one reads them over.

They both love the sound of beautiful sentences and the tinkle of rhyming words, and in fact, of the three great R's of life, they adore Reading and Riting, as much as they abhor 'Rithmetic.

The little girl in the old book is always thinking of what she is "going to be."

Uncle Jerry Cobb spoiled me a good deal in this direction. I remember he said to everybody when I wrote my verses for the flag-raising: "Nary rung on the ladder o' fame but that child'll climb if you give her time!" — poor Uncle Jerry! He will be so disappointed in me as time goes on. And still he would think I have already climbed two rungs on the ladder, although it is only a little Wareham ladder, for I am one of the "Pilot" editors, the first "girl editor" — and I have taken a fifty dollar prize in composition and paid off the interest on a twelve hundred dollar mortgage with it.

> *"High is the rank we now possess,*
> *But higher we shall rise;*
> *Though what we shall hereafter be*
> *Is hid from mortal eyes."*

This hymn was sung in meeting the Sunday after my election, and Mr. Aladdin was there that day and looked across the aisle and smiled at me. Then he sent me a sheet of paper from Boston the next morning with just one verse in the middle of it.

> *"She made the cleverest people quite ashamed;*
> *And ev'n the good with inward envy groan,*
> *Finding themselves so very much exceeded,*
> *In their own way by all the things that she did."*

Miss Maxwell says it is Byron, and I wish I had thought of the last rhyme before Byron did; my rhymes are always so common.

I am too busy doing, nowadays, to give very much thought to being. Mr. Aladdin was teasing me one day about what he calls my "cast-off careers."

"What makes you aim at any mark in particular, Rebecca?" he asked, looking at Miss Maxwell and laughing. "Women never hit what they aim at, anyway; but if they shut their eyes and shoot in the air they generally find themselves in the bull's eye."

I think one reason that I have always dreamed of what I should be, when I grew up, was, that even before father died mother worried about the mortgage on the farm, and what would become of us if it were foreclosed.

It was hard on children to be brought up on a mortgage that way, but oh! it was harder still on poor dear mother, who had seven of us then to think of, and still has three at home to feed and clothe out of the farm.

Aunt Jane says I am young for my age, Aunt Miranda is afraid that I will never really "grow up," Mr. Aladdin says that I don't know the world any better than the pearl inside of the oyster. They none of them know the old, old thoughts I have, some of them going back years and years; for they are never ones that I can speak about.

I remember how we children used to admire father, he was so handsome and graceful and amusing, never cross like mother, or too busy to play with us. He never did any work at home because he had to keep his hands nice for playing the church melodeon, or the violin or piano for dances.

Mother used to say: "Hannah and Rebecca, you must hull the strawberries, your father cannot help." "John, you must milk next year for I haven't the time and it would spoil your father's hands."

All the other men in Temperance village wore calico, or flannel shirts, except on Sundays, but Father never wore any but white ones with starched bosoms. He was very particular about them and mother used to stitch and stitch on the pleats, and press and press the bosoms and collar and cuffs, sometimes late at night.

Then she was tired and thin and gray, with no time to sew on new dresses for herself, and no time to wear them, because she was always taking care of the babies; and father was happy and well and handsome. But we children never thought much about it until once, after father had mortgaged the farm, there was going to be a sociable in Temperance village. Mother could not go as Jenny had whooping-cough and Mark had just broken his arm, and when she was tying father's necktie, the last thing before he started, he said: "I wish, Aurelia, that you cared a little about *your* appearance and *your* dress; it goes a long way with a man like me."

Mother had finished the tie, and her hands dropped suddenly.

153

I looked at her eyes and mouth while she looked at father and in a minute I was ever so old, with a grown-up ache in my heart. It has always stayed there, although I admired my handsome father and was proud of him because he was so talented; but now that I am older and have thought about things, my love for mother is different from what it used to be. Father was always the favorite when we were little, he was so interesting, and I wonder sometimes if we don't remember interesting people longer and better than we do those who are just good and patient. If so it seems very cruel.

As I look back I see that Miss Ross, the artist who brought me my pink parasol from Paris, sowed the first seeds in me of ambition to do something special. Her life seemed so beautiful and so easy to a child. I had not been to school then, or read George Macdonald, so I did not know that "Ease is the lovely result of forgotten toil."

Miss Ross sat out of doors and painted lovely things, and everybody said how wonderful they were, and bought them straight away; and she took care of a blind father and two brothers, and traveled wherever she wished. It comes back to me now, that summer when I was ten and Miss Ross painted me sitting by the mill-wheel while she talked to me of foreign countries!

The other day Miss Maxwell read something from Browning's poems to the girls of her literature class. It was about David the shepherd boy who used to lie in his hollow watching one eagle "wheeling slow as in sleep." He used to wonder about the wide world that the eagle beheld, the eagle that was stretching his wings so far up in the blue, while he, the poor shepherd boy, could see only the "strip twixt the hill and the sky;" for he lay in a hollow.

I told Mr. Baxter about it the next day, which was the Saturday before I joined the church. I asked him if it was wicked to long to see as much as the eagle saw?

There was never anybody quite like Mr. Baxter. "Rebecca dear," he said, "it may be that you need not always lie in a hollow, as the shepherd boy did; but wherever you lie, that little strip you see 'twixt the hill and the sky' is able to hold all of earth and all of heaven, if only you have the right sort of vision."

I was a long, long time about "experiencing religion." I remember Sunday afternoons at the brick house the first winter after I went there; when I used to sit in the middle of the dining-room as I was bid, silent and still, with the big family Bible on my knees. Aunt Miranda had Baxter's "Saints' Rest," but her seat was by the window, and she at least could give a glance into the street now and then without being positively wicked.

Aunt Jane used to read the "Pilgrim's Progress." The fire burned low; the tall clock ticked, ticked, so slowly and steadily, that the pictures swam before my eyes and I almost fell asleep.

They thought by shutting everything else out that I should see God; but I didn't, not once. I was so homesick for Sunnybook and John that I could hardly learn my weekly hymns, especially the sad, long one beginning:

> "My thoughts on awful subjects roll,
> Damnation and the dead."

It was brother John for whom I was chiefly homesick on Sunday afternoons, because at Sunnybrook Farm father was dead and mother was always busy, and Hannah never liked to talk.

Then the next year the missionaries from Syria came to Riverboro; and at the meeting Mr. Burch saw me playing the melodeon, and thought I was grown up and a church member, and so he asked me to lead in prayer.

I didn't dare to refuse, and when I prayed, which was just like thinking out loud, I found I could talk to God a great deal easier than to Aunt Miranda or even to Uncle Jerry Cobb. There were things I could say to Him that I could never say to anybody else, and saying them always made me happy and contented.

When Mr. Baxter asked me last year about joining the church, I told him I was afraid I did not understand God quite well enough to be a real member.

"So you don't quite understand God, Rebecca?" he asked, smiling. "Well, there is something else much more important, which is, that He understands you! He understands your feeble love, your longings, desires, hopes, faults, ambitions, crosses; and that, after all, is what counts! Of course you don't understand Him! You are overshadowed by His love, His power, His benignity, His

155

wisdom; that is as it should be! Why, Rebecca, dear, if you could stand erect and unabashed in God's presence, as one who perfectly comprehended His nature or His purposes, it would be sacrilege! Don't be puzzled out of your blessed inheritance of faith, my child; accept God easily and naturally, just as He accepts you!"

"God never puzzled me, Mr. Baxter; it isn't that," I said; "but the doctrines do worry me dreadfully."

"Let them alone for the present," Mr Baxter said. "Anyway, Rebecca, you can never prove God; you can only find Him!"

"Then do you think I have really experienced religion, Mr. Baxter?" I asked. "Am I the beginnings of a Christian?"

"You are a dear child of the understanding God!" Mr. Baxter said; "and I say it over to myself night and morning so that I can never forget it."

. . . .

The year is nearly over and the next few months will be lived in the rush and whirlwind of work that comes before graduation. The bell for philosophy class will ring in ten minutes, and as I have been writing for nearly two hours, I must learn my lesson going up the Academy hill. It will not be the first time; it is a grand hill for learning! I suppose after fifty years or so the very ground has become soaked with knowledge, and every particle of air in the vicinity is crammed with useful information.

I will put my book into my trunk (having no blessed haymow hereabouts) and take it out again,—when shall I take it out again?

After graduation perhaps I shall be too grown up and too busy to write in a Thought Book; but oh, if only something would happen worth putting down; something strange; something unusual; something different from the things that happen every day in Riverboro and Edgewood!

Graduation will surely take me a little out of "the hollow," — make me a little more like the soaring eagle, gazing at the whole wide world beneath him while he wheels "slow as in sleep." But whether or not, I'll try not to be a discontented shepherd, but remember what Mr. Baxter said, that the little strip that I see "twixt the hill and the sky" is able to hold all of earth and all of heaven, if only I have the eyes to see it.

Rebecca Rowena Randall.
Wareham Female Seminary, December 187—.

ELEVENTH CHRONICLE

ABIJAH THE BRAVE AND THE FAIR
EMMAJANE

I

"A warrior so bold and a maiden so bright
Conversed as they sat on the green.
They gazed at each other in tender delight.
Alonzo the brave was the name of the knight,
And the maid was the fair Imogene.

"Alas!' said the youth, 'since tomorrow I go
To fight in a far distant land,
Your tears for my absence soon ceasing to flow,
Some other will court you, and you will bestow
On a wealthier suitor your hand.'

'Oh, hush these suspicions!' Fair Imogene said,
"So hurtful to love and to me!
For if you be living, or if you be dead,
I swear by the Virgin that none in your stead
Shall the husband of Imogene be!'

Ever since she was eight years old Rebecca had wished to be eighteen, but now that she was within a month of that awe-inspiring and long-desired age she wondered if, after all, it was destined to be a turning point in her quiet existence. Her eleventh year, for instance, had been a real turning-point, since it was then that she had left Sunnybrook Farm and come to her maiden aunts in Riverboro. Aurelia Randall may have been doubtful as to the effect upon her spinster sisters of the irrepressible child, but she

158

was hopeful from the first that the larger opportunities of Riverboro would be the "making" of Rebecca herself.

The next turning-point was her fourteenth year, when she left the district school for the Wareham Female Seminary, then in the hey-day of its local fame. Graduation (next to marriage, perhaps, the most thrilling episode in the life of a little country girl) happened at seventeen, and not long afterward her Aunt Miranda's death, sudden and unexpected, changed not only all the outward activities and conditions of her life, but played its own part in her development.

The brick house looked very homelike and pleasant on a June morning nowadays with children's faces smiling at the windows and youthful footsteps sounding through the halls; and the brass knocker on the red-painted front door might have remembered Rebecca's prayer of a year before, when she leaned against its sun-warmed brightness and whispered: "God bless Aunt Miranda; God bless the brick house that was; God bless the brick house that's going to be!"

All the doors and blinds were open to the sun and air as they had never been in Miss Miranda Sawyer's time. The hollyhock bed that had been her chief pride was never neglected, and Rebecca liked to hear the neighbors say that there was no such row of beautiful plants and no such variety of beautiful colors in Riverboro as those that climbed up and peeped in at the kitchen windows where old Miss Miranda used to sit.

Now that the place was her very own Rebecca felt a passion of pride in its smoothly mown fields, its carefully thinned-out woods, its blooming garden spots, and its well-weeded vegetable patch; felt, too whenever she looked at any part of it, a passion of gratitude to the stern old aunt who had looked upon her as the future head of the family, as well as a passion of desire to be worthy of that trust.

It had been a very difficult year for a girl fresh from school: the death of her aunt, the nursing of Miss Jane, prematurely enfeebled by the shock, the removal of her own invalid mother and the rest of the little family from Sunnybrook Farm. But all had gone smoothly;

and when once the Randall fortunes had taken an upward turn nothing seemed able to stop their intrepid ascent.

Aurelia Randall renewed her youth in the companionship of her sister Jane and the comforts by which her children were surrounded; the mortgage was no longer a daily terror, for Sunnybrook had been sold to the new railroad; Hannah, now Mrs. Will Melville, was happily situated; John, at last, was studying medicine; Mark, the boisterous and unlucky brother, had broken no bones for several months; while Jenny and Fanny were doing well at the district school under Miss Libby Moses, Miss Dearborn's successor.

"I don't feel very safe," thought Rebecca, remembering all these unaccustomed mercies as she sat on the front doorsteps, with her tatting shuttle flying in and out of the fine cotton like a hummingbird. "It's just like one of those too beautiful July days that winds up with a thundershower before night! Still, when you remember that the Randalls never had anything but thunder and lightning, rain, snow, and hail, in their family history for twelve or fifteen years, perhaps it is only natural that they should enjoy a little spell of settled weather. If it really turns out to BE settled, now that Aunt Jane and mother are strong again I must be looking up one of what Mr. Aladdin calls my cast-off careers." — "There comes Emma Jane Perkins through her front gate; she will be here in a minute, and I'll tease her!" and Rebecca ran in the door and seated herself at the old piano that stood between the open windows in the parlor.

Peeping from behind the muslin curtains, she waited until Emma Jane was on the very threshold and then began singing her version of an old ballad, made that morning while she was dressing. The ballad was a great favorite of hers, and she counted on doing telling execution with it in the present instance by the simple subterfuge of removing the original hero and heroine, Alonzo and Imogene, and substituting Abijah the Brave and the Fair Emmajane, leaving the circumstances in the first three verses unaltered, because in truth they seemed to require no alteration.

Her high, clear voice, quivering with merriment, floated through the windows into the still summer air:

160

"'A warrior so bold and a maiden so bright
Conversed as they sat on the green.
They gazed at each other in tender delight.
Abijah the Brave was the name of the knight,
And the maid was the Fair Emmajane.'"

"Rebecca Randall, stop! Somebody'll hear you!"

"No, they won't—they're making jelly in the kitchen, miles away."

"'Alas!' said the youth, since tomorrow I go
To fight in a far distant land,
Your tears for my absence soon ceasing to flow,
Some other will court you, and you will bestow
On a wealthier suitor your hand.'"

"Rebecca, you can't *think* how your voice carries! I believe mother can hear it over to my house!"

"Then, if she can, I must sing the third verse, just to clear your reputation from the cloud cast upon it in the second," laughed her tormentor, going on with the song:

"'Oh, hush these suspicions!' Fair Emmajane said, 'So hurtful to love and to me! For if you be living, or if you be dead, I swear, my Abijah, that none in your stead, Shall the husband of Emmajane be!'"

After ending the third verse Rebecca wheeled around on the piano stool and confronted her friend, who was carefully closing the parlor windows:—

"Emma Jane Perkins, it is an ordinary Thursday afternoon at four o'clock and you have on your new blue barege, although there is not even a church sociable in prospect this evening. What does this mean? Is Abijah the Brave coming at last?"

"I don't know certainly, but it will be some time this week."

"And of course you'd rather be dressed up and not seen, than seen when not dressed up. Right, my Fair Emmajane; so would I. Not that it makes any difference to poor me, wearing my fourth best black and white calico and expecting nobody.

161

"Oh, well, *you*! There's something inside of you that does instead of pretty dresses," cried Emma Jane, whose adoration of her friend had never altered nor lessened since they met at the age of eleven. "You know you are as different from anybody else in Riverboro as a princess in a fairy story. Libby Moses says they would notice you in Lowell, Massachusetts!"

"Would they? I wonder," speculated Rebecca, rendered almost speechless by this tribute to her charms. "Well, if Lowell, Massachusetts, could see me, or if you could see me, in my new lavender muslin with the violet sash, it would die of envy, and so would you!"

"If I had been going to be envious of you, Rebecca, I should have died years ago. Come, let's go out on the steps where it's shady and cool."

"And where we can see the Perkins front gate and the road running both ways," teased Rebecca, and then, softening her tone, she said: "How is it getting on, Emmy? Tell me what's happened since I've been in Brunswick."

"Nothing much," confessed Emma Jane. "He writes to me, but I don't write to him, you know. I don't dare to, till he comes to the house."

"Are his letters still in Latin?" asked Rebecca, with a twinkling eye.

"Oh, no! Not now, because—well, because there are things you can't seem to write in Latin. I saw him at the Masonic picnic in the grove, but he won't say anything *real* to me till he gets more pay and dares to speak to mother and father. He *is* brave in all other ways, but I ain't sure he'll ever have the courage for that, he's so afraid of them and always has been. Just remember what's in his mind all the time, Rebecca, that my folks know all about what his mother was, and how he was born on the poor-farm. Not that I care; look how he's educated and worked himself up! I think he's perfectly elegant, and I shouldn't mind if he had been born in the bulrushes, like Moses."

Emma Jane's every-day vocabulary was pretty much what it had been before she went to the expensive Wareham Female Seminary. She had acquired a certain amount of information

162

concerning the art of speech, but in moments of strong feeling she lapsed into the vernacular. She grew slowly in all directions, did Emma Jane, and, to use Rebecca's favorite nautilus figure, she had left comparatively few outgrown shells on the shores of "life's unresting sea."

"Moses wasn't born in the bulrushes, Emmy dear," corrected Rebecca laughingly. "Pharaoh's daughter found him there. It wasn't quite as romantic a scene—Squire Bean's wife taking little Abijah Flagg from the poorhouse when his girl-mother died, but, oh, I think Abijah's splendid! Mr. Ladd says Riverboro'll be proud of him yet, and I shouldn't wonder, Emmy dear, if you had a three-story house with a cupola on it, some day; and sitting down at your mahogany desk inlaid with garnets, you will write notes stating that Mrs. Abijah Flagg requests the pleasure of Miss Rebecca Randall's company to tea, and that the Hon. Abijah Flagg, M.C., will call for her on his way from the station with a span of horses and the turquoise carryall!"

Emma Jane laughed at the ridiculous prophecy, and answered: "If I ever write the invitation I shan't be addressing it to Miss Randall, I'm sure of that; it'll be to Mrs. — —"

"Don't!" cried Rebecca impetuously, changing color and putting her hand over Emma Jane's lips. "If you won't I'll stop teasing. I couldn't bear a name put to anything, I couldn't, Emmy dear! I wouldn't tease you, either, if it weren't something we've both known ever so long—something that you have always consulted me about of your own accord, and Abijah too."

"Don't get excited," replied Emma Jane, "I was only going to say you were sure to be Mrs. Somebody in course of time."

"Oh," said Rebecca with a relieved sigh, her color coming back; "if that's all you meant, just nonsense; but I thought, I thought—I don't really know just what I thought!"

"I think you thought something you didn't want me to think you thought," said Emma Jane with unusual felicity.

"No, it's not that; but somehow, today, I have been remembering things. Perhaps it was because at breakfast Aunt Jane and mother reminded me of my coming birthday and said that Squire Bean would give me the deed of the brick house. That made

163

me feel very old and responsible; and when I came out on the steps this afternoon it was just as if pictures of the old years were moving up and down the road. Everything is so beautiful today! Doesn't the sky look as if it had been dyed blue and the fields painted pink and green and yellow this very minute?"

"It's a perfectly elegant day!" responded Emma Jane with a sigh. "If only my mind was at rest! That's the difference between being young and grown-up. We never used to think and worry."

"Indeed we didn't! Look, Emmy, there's the very spot where Uncle Jerry Cobb stopped the stage and I stepped out with my pink parasol and my bouquet of purple lilacs, and you were watching me from your bedroom window and wondering what I had in mother's little hair trunk strapped on behind. Poor Aunt Miranda didn't love me at first sight, and oh, how cross she was the first two years! But now every hard thought I ever had comes back to me and cuts like a knife!"

"She was dreadful hard to get along with, and I used to hate her like poison," confessed Emma Jane; "but I am sorry now. She was kinder toward the last, anyway, and then, you see children know so little! We never suspected she was sick or that she was worrying over that lost interest money."

"That's the trouble. People seem hard and unreasonable and unjust, and we can't help being hurt at the time, but if they die we forget everything but our own angry speeches; somehow we never remember theirs. And oh, Emma Jane, there's another such a sweet little picture out there in the road. The next day after I came to Riverboro, do you remember, I stole out of the brick house crying, and leaned against the front gate. You pushed your little fat pink-and-white face through the pickets and said: Don't cry! I'll kiss you if you will me!'"

Lumps rose suddenly in Emma Jane's throat, and she put her arm around Rebecca's waist as they sat together side by side.

"Oh, I do remember," she said in a choking voice. "And I can see the two of us driving over to North Riverboro and selling soap to Mr. Adam Ladd; and lighting up the premium banquet lamp at the Simpson party; and laying the daisies round Jacky Winslow's mother when she was dead in the cabin; and trundling Jacky up and down the street in our old baby carriage!"

"And I remember you," continued Rebecca, "being chased down the hill by Jacob Moody, when we were being Daughters of Zion and you had been chosen to convert him!"

"And I remember you, getting the flag back from Mr. Simpson; and how you looked when you spoke your verses at the flag-raising."

"And have you forgotten the week I refused to speak to Abijah Flagg because he fished my turban with the porcupine quills out of the river when I hoped at last that I had lost it! Oh, Emma Jane, we had dear good times together in the little harbor.'"

"I always thought that was an elegant composition of yours — that farewell to the class," said Emma Jane.

"The strong tide bears us on, out of the little harbor of childhood into the unknown seas," recalled Rebecca. "It is bearing you almost out of my sight, Emmy, these last days, when you put on a new dress in the afternoon and look out of the window instead of coming across the street. Abijah Flagg never used to be in the little harbor with the rest of us; when did he first sail in, Emmy?"

Emma Jane grew a deeper pink and her button-hole of a mouth quivered with delicious excitement.

"It was last year at the seminary, when he wrote me his first Latin letter from Limerick Academy," she said in a half whisper.

"I remember," laughed Rebecca. "You suddenly began the study of the dead languages, and the Latin dictionary took the place of the crochet needle in your affections. It was cruel of you never to show me that letter, Emmy!"

"I know every word of it by heart," said the blushing Emma Jane, "and I think I really ought to say it to you, because it's the only way you will ever know how perfectly elegant Abijah is. Look the other way, Rebecca. Shall I have to translate it for you, do you think, because it seems to me I could not bear to do that!"

"It depends upon Abijah's Latin and your pronunciation," teased Rebecca. "Go on; I will turn my eyes toward the orchard."

The Fair Emmajane, looking none too old still for the "little harbor," but almost too young for the "unknown seas," gathered up

165

her courage and recited like a tremulous parrot the boyish love letter that had so fired her youthful imagination.

"Vale, carissima, carissima puella!" repeated Rebecca in her musical voice. "Oh, how beautiful it sounds! I don't wonder it altered your feeling for Abijah! Upon my word, Emma Jane," she cried with a sudden change of tone, "if I had suspected for an instant that Abijah the Brave had that Latin letter in him I should have tried to get him to write it to me; and then it would be I who would sit down at my mahogany desk and ask Miss Perkins to come to tea with Mrs. Flagg."

Emma Jane paled and shuddered openly. "I speak as a church member, Rebecca," she said, "when I tell you I've always thanked the Lord that you never looked at Abijah Flagg and he never looked at you. If either of you ever had, there never would have been a chance for me, and I've always known it!"

II

The romance alluded to in the foregoing chapter had been going on, so far as Abijah Flagg's part of it was concerned, for many years, his affection dating back in his own mind to the first moment that he saw Emma Jane Perkins at the age of nine.

Emma Jane had shown no sign of reciprocating his attachment until the last three years, when the evolution of the chore-boy into the budding scholar and man of affairs had inflamed even her somewhat dull imagination.

Squire Bean's wife had taken Abijah away from the poorhouse, thinking that she could make him of some little use in her home. Abbie Flagg, the mother, was neither wise nor beautiful; it is to be feared that she was not even good, and her lack of all these desirable qualities, particularly the last one, had been impressed upon the child ever since he could remember. People seemed to blame him for being in the world at all; this world that had not expected him nor desired him, nor made any provision for him. The great battle-axe of poorhouse opinion was forever leveled at the mere little atom of innocent transgression, until he grew sad and shy, clumsy, stiff, and self-conscious. He had an indomitable craving for love in his heart and had never received a caress in his life.

He was more contented when he came to Squire Bean's house. The first year he could only pick up chips, carry pine wood into the kitchen, go to the post-office, run errands, drive the cows, and feed the hens, but every day he grew more and more useful.

His only friend was little Jim Watson, the storekeeper's son, and they were inseparable companions whenever Abijah had time for play.

One never-to-be-forgotten July day a new family moved into the white cottage between Squire Bean's house and the Sawyers'. Mr. Perkins had sold his farm beyond North Riverboro and had established a blacksmith's shop in the village, at the Edgewood end of the bridge. This fact was of no special interest to the nine-year-old Abijah, but what really was of importance, was the appearance of a pretty little girl of seven in the front yard; a pretty little fat doll of a girl, with bright fuzzy hair, pink cheeks, blue eyes, and a smile of almost bewildering continuity. Another might have criticised it as having the air of being glued on, but Abijah was already in the toils and never wished it to move.

The next day being the glorious Fourth and a holiday, Jimmy Watson came over like David, to visit his favorite Jonathan. His Jonathan met him at the top of the hill, pleaded a pressing engagement, curtly sent him home, and then went back to play with his new idol, with whom he had already scraped acquaintance, her parents being exceedingly busy settling the new house.

After the noon dinner Jimmy again yearned to resume friendly relations, and, forgetting his rebuff, again toiled up the hill and appeared unexpectedly at no great distance from the Perkins premises, wearing the broad and beaming smile of one who is confident of welcome.

His morning call had been officious and unpleasant and unsolicited, but his afternoon visit could only be regarded as impudent, audacious, and positively dangerous; for Abijah and

Emma Jane were cosily playing house, the game of all others in which it is particularly desirable to have two and not three participants.

At that moment the nature of Abijah changed, at once and forever. Without a pang of conscience he flew over the intervening patch of ground between himself and his dreaded rival, and seizing small stones and larger ones, as haste and fury demanded, flung them at Jimmy Watson, and flung and flung, till the bewildered boy ran down the hill howling. Then he made a "stickin'" door to the play-house, put the awed Emma Jane inside and strode up and down in front of the edifice like an Indian brave. At such an early age does woman become a distracting and disturbing influence in man's career!

Time went on, and so did the rivalry between the poorhouse boy and the son of wealth, but Abijah's chances of friendship with Emma Jane grew fewer and fewer as they both grew older. He did not go to school, so there was no meeting-ground there, but sometimes, when he saw the knot of boys and girls returning in the afternoon, he would invite Elijah and Elisha, the Simpson twins, to visit him, and take pains to be in Squire Bean's front yard, doing something that might impress his inamorata as she passed the premises.

As Jimmy Watson was particularly small and fragile, Abijah generally chose feats of strength and skill for these prearranged performances.

Sometimes he would throw his hat up into the elm trees as far as he could and, when it came down, catch it on his head. Sometimes he would walk on his hands, with his legs wriggling in the air, or turn a double somersault, or jump incredible distances across the extended arms of the Simpson twins; and his bosom swelled with pride when the girls exclaimed, "Isn't he splendid!" although he often heard his rival murmur scornfully, *"Smarty Aleck!"* — a scathing allusion of unknown origin.

Squire Bean, although he did not send the boy to school (thinking, as he was of no possible importance in the universe, it was not worth while bothering about his education), finally became impressed with his ability, lent him books, and gave him more time

168

to study. These were all he needed, books and time, and when there was an especially hard knot to untie, Rebecca, as the star scholar of the neighborhood, helped him to untie it.

When he was sixteen he longed to go away from Riverboro and be something better than a chore boy. Squire Bean had been giving him small wages for three or four years, and when the time of parting came presented him with a ten-dollar bill and a silver watch.

Many a time had he discussed his future with Rebecca and asked her opinion.

This was not strange, for there was nothing in human form that she could not and did not converse with, easily and delightedly. She had ideas on every conceivable subject, and would have cheerfully advised the minister if he had asked her. The fishman consulted her when he couldn't endure his mother-in-law another minute in the house; Uncle Jerry Cobb didn't part with his river field until he had talked it over with Rebecca; and as for Aunt Jane, she couldn't decide whether to wear her black merino or her gray thibet unless Rebecca cast the final vote.

Abijah wanted to go far away from Riverboro, as far as Limerick Academy, which was at least fifteen miles; but although this seemed extreme, Rebecca agreed, saying pensively: "There IS a kind of magicness about going far away and then coming back all changed."

This was precisely Abijah's unspoken thought. Limerick knew nothing of Abbie Flagg's worthlessness, birth, and training, and the awful stigma of his poorhouse birth, so that he would start fair. He could have gone to Wareham and thus remained within daily sight of the beloved Emma Jane; but no, he was not going to permit her to watch him in the process of "becoming," but after he had "become" something. He did not propose to take any risks after all these years of silence and patience. Not he! He proposed to disappear, like the moon on a dark night, and as he was, at present, something that Mr. Perkins would by no means have in the family nor Mrs. Perkins allow in the house, he would neither return to Riverboro nor ask any favors of them until he had something to offer. Yes, sir. He was going to be crammed to the eyebrows with

169

learning for one thing,—useless kinds and all,—going to have good clothes, and a good income. Everything that was in his power should be right, because there would always be lurking in the background the things he never could help—the mother and the poorhouse.

So he went away, and, although at Squire Bean's invitation he came back the first year for two brief visits at Christmas and Easter, he was little seen in Riverboro, for Mr. Ladd finally found him a place where he could make his vacations profitable and learn bookkeeping at the same time.

The visits in Riverboro were tantalizing rather than pleasant. He was invited to two parties, but he was all the time conscious of his shirt-collar, and he was sure that his "pants" were not the proper thing, for by this time his ideals of dress had attained an almost unrealizable height. As for his shoes, he felt that he walked on carpets as if they were furrows and he were propelling a plow or a harrow before him. They played Drop the Handkerchief and Copenhagen at the parties, but he had not had the audacity to kiss Emma Jane, which was bad enough, but Jimmy had and did, which was infinitely worse! The sight of James Watson's unworthy and over-ambitious lips on Emma Jane's pink cheek almost destroyed his faith in an overruling Providence.

After the parties were over he went back to his old room in Squire Bean's shed chamber. As he lay in bed his thoughts fluttered about Emma Jane as swallows circle around the eaves. The terrible sickness of hopeless handicapped love kept him awake. Once he crawled out of bed in the night, lighted the lamp, and looked for his mustache, remembering that he had seen a suspicion of down on his rival's upper lip. He rose again half an hour later, again lighted the lamp, put a few drops of oil on his hair, and brushed it violently for several minutes. Then he went back to bed, and after making up his mind that he would buy a dulcimer and learn to play on it so that he would be more attractive at parties, and outshine his rival in society as he had aforetime in athletics, he finally sank into a troubled slumber.

Those days, so full of hope and doubt and torture, seemed mercifully unreal now, they lay so far back in the past—six or eight years, in fact, which is a lifetime to the lad of twenty—and meantime he had conquered many of the adverse circumstances that had threatened to cloud his career.

Abijah Flagg was a true child of his native State. Something of the same timber that Maine puts into her forests, something of the same strength and resisting power that she works into her rocks, goes into her sons and daughters; and at twenty Abijah was going to take his fate in his hand and ask Mr. Perkins, the rich blacksmith, if, after a suitable period of probation (during which he would further prepare himself for his exalted destiny), he might marry the fair Emma Jane, sole heiress of the Perkins house and fortunes.

III

This was boy and girl love, calf love, perhaps, though even that may develop into something larger, truer, and finer; but not so far away were other and very different hearts growing and budding, each in its own way. There was little Miss Dearborn, the pretty school teacher, drifting into a foolish alliance because she did not agree with her stepmother at home; there was Herbert Dunn, valedictorian of his class, dazzled by Huldah Meserve, who like a glowworm "shone afar off bright, but looked at near, had neither heat nor light."

There was sweet Emily Maxwell, less than thirty still, with most of her heart bestowed in the wrong quarter. She was toiling on at the Wareham school, living as unselfish a life as a nun in a convent; lavishing the mind and soul of her, the heart and body of her, on her chosen work. How many women give themselves thus, consciously and unconsciously; and, though they themselves miss the joys and compensations of mothering their own little twos and threes, God must be grateful to them for their mothering of the hundreds which make them so precious in His regenerating purposes.

Then there was Adam Ladd, waiting at thirty-five for a girl to

171

grow a little older, simply because he could not find one already grown who suited his somewhat fastidious and exacting tastes.

"I'll not call Rebecca perfection," he quoted once, in a letter to Emily Maxwell, — "I'll not call her perfection, for that's a post, afraid to move. But she's a dancing sprig of the tree next it."

When first she appeared on his aunt's piazza in North Riverboro and insisted on selling him a large quantity of very inferior soap in order that her friends, the Simpsons, might possess a premium in the shape of a greatly needed banquet lamp, she had riveted his attention. He thought all the time that he enjoyed talking with her more than with any woman alive, and he had never changed his opinion. She always caught what he said as if it were a ball tossed to her, and sometimes her mind, as through it his thoughts came back to him, seemed like a prism which had dyed them with deeper colors.

Adam Ladd always called Rebecca in his heart his little Spring. His boyhood had been lonely and unhappy. That was the part of life he had missed, and although it was the full summer of success and prosperity with him now, he found his lost youth only in her.

She was to him — how shall I describe it?

Do you remember an early day in May with budding leaf, warm earth, tremulous air, and changing, willful sky — how new it seemed? How fresh and joyous beyond all explaining?

Have you lain with half-closed eyes where the flickering of sunlight through young leaves, the song of birds and brook and the fragrance of wild flowers combined to charm your senses, and you felt the sweetness and grace of nature as never before?

Rebecca was springtide to Adam's thirsty heart. She was blithe youth incarnate; she was music — an Aeolian harp that every passing breeze woke to some whispering little tune; she was a changing, iridescent joy-bubble; she was the shadow of a leaf dancing across a dusty floor. No bough of his thought could be so bare but she somehow built a nest in it and evoked life where none was before.

And Rebecca herself?

She had been quite unconscious of all this until very lately, and even now she was but half awakened; searching among her childish

172

instincts and her girlish dreams for some Ariadne thread that should guide her safely through the labyrinth of her new sensations.

For the moment she was absorbed, or thought she was, in the little love story of Abijah and Emma Jane, but in reality, had she realized it, that love story served chiefly as a basis of comparison for a possible one of her own, later on.

She liked and respected Abijah Flagg, and loving Emma Jane was a habit contracted early in life; but everything that they did or said, or thought or wrote, or hoped or feared, seemed so inadequate, so painfully short of what might be done or said, or thought or written, or hoped or feared, under easily conceivable circumstances, that she almost felt a disposition to smile gently at the fancy of the ignorant young couple that they had caught a glimpse of the great vision.

She was sitting under the sweet apple tree at twilight. Supper was over; Mark's restless feet were quiet, Fanny and Jenny were tucked safely in bed; her aunt and her mother were stemming currants on the side porch.

A blue spot at one of the Perkins windows showed that in one vestal bosom hope was not dead yet, although it was seven o'clock.

Suddenly there was the sound of a horse's feet coming up the quiet road; plainly a steed hired from some metropolis like Milltown or Wareham, as Riverboro horses when through with their day's work never disported themselves so gayly.

A little open vehicle came in sight, and in it sat Abijah Flagg. The wagon was so freshly painted and so shiny that Rebecca thought that he must have alighted at the bridge and given it a last polish. The creases in his trousers, too, had an air of having been pressed in only a few minutes before. The whip was new and had a yellow ribbon on it; the gray suit of clothes was new, and the coat flourished a flower in its button-hole. The hat was the latest thing in hats, and the intrepid swain wore a seal-ring on the little finger of his right hand. As Rebecca remembered that she had guided it in making capital G's in his copy-book, she felt positively maternal, although she was two years younger than Abijah the Brave.

He drove up to the Perkins gate and was so long about hitching

173

the horse that Rebecca's heart beat tumultuously at the thought of Emma Jane's heart waiting under the blue barege. Then he brushed an imaginary speck off his sleeve, then he drew on a pair of buff kid gloves, then he went up the path, rapped at the knocker, and went in.

"Not all the heroes go to the wars," thought Rebecca. "Abijah has laid the ghost of his father and redeemed the memory of his mother, for no one will dare say again that Abbie Flagg's son could never amount to anything!"

The minutes went by, and more minutes, and more. The tranquil dusk settled down over the little village street and the young moon came out just behind the top of the Perkins pine tree.

The Perkins front door opened and Abijah the Brave came out hand in hand with his Fair Emma Jane.

They walked through the orchard, the eyes of the old couple following them from the window, and just as they disappeared down the green slope that led to the riverside the gray coat sleeve encircled the blue barege waist.

Rebecca, quivering with instant sympathy and comprehension, hid her face in her hands.

"Emmy has sailed away and I am all alone in the little harbor," she thought.

It was as if childhood, like a thing real and visible, were slipping down the grassy river banks, after Abijah and Emma Jane, and disappearing like them into the moon-lit shadows of the summer night.

"I am all alone in the little harbor," she repeated; "and oh, I wonder, I wonder, shall I be afraid to leave it, if anybody ever comes to carry me out to sea!"

THE END

174

Milton Keynes UK
Ingram Content Group UK Ltd.
UKHW042356070923
428219UK00003B/10/J

9 798888 306499